Chasing Maya

GLOBAL VISION PRESS

World Class Writings for Global Citizens

- **THE HANUMAN FACTOR** by **Anand Krishna** **(Self-Help)**
  (*Life Lessons from the Most Successful Spiritual CEO*)
- **REVERSE YOUR THOUGHTS, REVERSE YOUR DISEASES**
  (*Retracing Your Path back to Health*)
  by **Anil Bhatnagar** **(Self-Help)**
- **THE 10-POUND SHRED** by **Tommy Europe** **(Health & Fitness)**
  (*From Flab to Fit in 4 weeks*)
- **DEBT-FREE FOREVER** by **Gail Vaz-Oxlade** **(Personal Finance)**
  (*Take Control of Your Money and Your Life*)
- **THE LOST IDENTITY** by **Troy Bond** **(Fiction)**
  (*Quest for the Text of Akbar—The text which holds the key to the entire Christian Faith*)
- **TALE OF A WASTELAND** by **Phanishwar Nath 'Renu'** **(Fiction)**
  (*English version of highly acclaimed Hindi novel 'Parti:Parikatha'*)
- **THE GROWING YEARS** by **Ann Delorme** **(Fiction)**
  (*Incidents in the Life of a Family*)
- **FANTASIA** by **Vaughn Petterson** **(Fiction)**
  (*On a Theme of Thomas Tallis*)
- **CHASING MAYA** by **Rohan Gogoi** **(Fiction)**
  (*A Journey of Self-Discovery*)
- **THE GREAT HORIZON** by **Debabrata Dasgupta** **(Biographies)**
  (*Biography of Great Scientist, Sir Alexander Fleming*)
- **REALITY REPAIR** by **William Cottringer** **(Self Help)**
  (*Fixing a Lot by Knowing a Little*)
- **TURN YOUR LIFE AROUND WITH REIKI**
  (*The Complete Guide to the Science and Practice of Reiki*)
  by **Anil Bhatnagar** **(Self Help)**
- **SHAKE UP INDIA** by **Jayant V. Narlikar** **(Inspire)**
  (*The Need of the Times*)
- **THE CHANGE MAKER** by **Subhash Agrawal** **(Inspire)**
  (*A Crusade Through Letters*)
- **TIGER TANTRA** by **Ganga Prasad Vimal** **(Fiction)**
  (*English version of an unusual and highly acclaimed Hindi novel 'Mrigaantak'*)
- **SHE** by **Dixy Gandhi** **(Fiction)**
  (*Stories of Modern Indian Women*)
- **A CODER'S COCKTAIL!** by **Shashwat Rai** **(Fiction)**
  (*What not to do in IT...*)
- **THE KINDLING TOUCH** by **Debabrata Dasgupta** **(Biographies)**
  (*Biography of Madame Curie*)
- **THE LUCK OF THE JEWS** by **Michael Benanav** **(True Story)**
  (*A True Story of Love, Death and Survival in the Holocaust*)
- **THANK YOU, IDI AMIN** by **Mohezin Tejani** **(True Story)**
  (*A Memoir of the Asian Exodus*)

Chasing Maya

Rohan Gogoi

GLOBAL
VISION
PRESS

Published by Global Vision Press

ISBN 978-93-80707-36-5 (Flexi-Back)

GLOBAL VISION PRESS
4855/24, Ansari Road, Daryaganj
New Delhi-110002, India

This is a work of fiction. Names, characters, places and incidents are either the product of author's imagination or are used fictitiously and any resemblance to any actual person, living or dead, events or locales is entirely coincidental.

Typeset by
AJAY ARTS
New Delhi

Printed at Rashtriya Printers, Delhi

To the soul in pursuit of true happiness

Contents

1

Burden of Mediocrity

"HONEY, can you switch off the balcony lamps, please…?"

"…And what are you doing there, by the way? It's two-thirty honey… Don't you have to go to work tomorrow? You know it's a Monday, right?" …Aparoopa doesn't ever fail to remind….

A yet another tedious night spent in dire puzzlement and despair and I see the morning sun meekly rising behind the thin ashen clouds… Phew! Pune's weather can be unbelievably astonishing… I look through my bedroom window and feel vaguely lost…. Not quite sure if I would really want to go to work today!

I push myself off to the balcony and lit a cigarette... and suddenly a gush of wild thoughts overwhelms me from all around… Why don't I feel like going to work? Why do I hate my job? Why am I generally disinterested in things that I do? What is it that makes me feel incomplete though the world sees me as a fairly successful man? Why do I always feel that I am stuck and lagging behind? Why am I not happy in life?

"So Mr. Siddhartha Kumar, you didn't sleep the whole night?" Apu, I mean Aparoopa, sounds terribly annoyed.

"Fine, go ahead. Have a great Monday anyway!"

Honk! Honk! God… even these trifling traffic jams can be so irritating! Honk! Honk! Just one more traffic signal to cross and

I am there at my office parking – all set to start a yet another *eventful* week! Evident pretensions, pointless discussions and needless confrontations – that's the forecast for the week, as usual! In fact for the past nine years, life has ceaselessly been going through the same old stressful grind. Thank God, by now, I have somehow picked up the tactics to manage this world around; otherwise coming this far in my career wasn't really easy....

"Hey Sid...! What's up dude? How was weekend? Come on, you look so dull? Why *yaar*... What happened?"

One man, zillion questions! That's Ninad, my good old colleague; not quite popular among others in the company; but certainly my only friend at work. Actually, I have always liked him for his raw wit and blunt humour... and yes, there's another reason of course.... He's the only one around who can unmistakably read an otherwise subtle I-hate-Mondays look on my face! Phew... Mondays!

Beep...beep. The telephone operator speaks up, "Good Morning Sir, Kalra Sir's on the line."

God... this Kalra... won't even let me start my week in peace!

Bobby Kalra, my boss, the Chief Executive of the company is just another huge pain in my life... Workaholic, frustratingly meticulous, needlessly *process-oriented* and unfittingly flamboyant for his age, there's just one thing that I really like about him; that for no precise reason he just adores me.... This of course, at times forces me to succumb to unnecessary demands but by and large, his fondness for me has been to my benefit.

Oh, I haven't yet told you about what I do for my company, right? Well, a difficult one to answer! If you go by my business-card, my designation reads 'Senior Business Manager'. Though I was hired as a Business Development Executive for promoting the company in the emerging markets of Asia Pacific, due to an *evident* lack of global exposure, I was asked to operate from the India headquarters, *gain some experience* and *then* move to Sydney. Since then, seven years have passed and I am still here; juggled between roles and functions, appreciated for all the hard work and promoted more frequently than expected. Though couple of times, I did pick up the topic with the management about my proposed assignment in the Asia Pacific, their response was sufficiently convincing… "You are doing very well Siddhartha. We don't want to destabilise the existing set-up. Aren't you happy with the kind of growth you have achieved here?"

So, today I am one of the seventeen senior managers in the company – not too bad a thing to be in a thousand people organization!

Though, going by my designation, I am expected to do something more serious and strategic, I normally spend most of my time setting up processes for Sales, Marketing, Communication and Support teams. My job, as of today, is largely about setting alarms, sending reminders, following up with people and calling for review meetings. And I must tell you, I do it really well!

But now I can foresee a temporary change in my role. There's a new agenda in hand: Kalra wants us to think creatively, and more importantly, I need to create a process to make that happen!

"But, dude, how can you create a process for others to think creatively?" That's Ninad again. But honestly, I don't care! In fact, I am more than convinced that like many of those countless whimsical propositions this too would soon be swept away quietly from the floors of the organisation.

But on second thoughts, will there ever be an end to these nonsensical demands? In the last nine years of my career, I have worked hysterically on an endless list of assignments varying in sorts, complexities and magnitude. But I genuinely wonder if anything that I have done as part of these assignments can ever be called worthwhile. And as I reassess my career so far, I am just left with the thought that I have never ever been part of anything that has made even the slightest of an impact to the world or for that matter, to the tiniest fraction of it! God! What am I doing? …Why am I living such a dead life…? I definitely deserve more excitement and happiness and I guess I must do something about it….

"Sid *yaar;* what's wrong with you dude? It's one-thirty *yaar*, come on, let's go for lunch." Ninad and I normally go out for lunch together. Crazy creature; he has to get his day's quota of *Roasted Malabar Chicken*!

"You must tell me today…! You really look depressed dude… Sick of Kalra, hah? Tell me dude…." He wouldn't stop.

But, what do I tell him? Do I really know, what's bothering me? I say I am fine, Kalra's fine, the job's fine, the company's fine, but then what's wrong?

May be, I am bored of this monotony. May be, I need a change…. Every day's the same, every week's the same, and all my weekends are the same! Apu would say it's no big deal – that's how the Indian middle class lives!

"Yes dude, tell me what's wrong?" Ninad refuses to give up.

I think what's bothering me these days is probably the realisation that of late I am just living a life of despair, disgust and dire insignificance.

"Okay, that's quite a confession", Ninad exclaims impishly.

In fact, I just couldn't sleep last night… I was thinking about it for quite a while... and I realised that I am slowly losing the zeal which has pushed me this far in my career. I don't feel motivated enough… I feel like taking a break from work and spend a long holiday in some quiet corner of the world.

"Honey, Riya just called up… They are planning a trip to Konkan next weekend and wanted us to join them. I said yes; okay *na*?" Apu…! She would always commit and then ask. But this time; I have to say *no*. Enough of these trips with strangers! After all how can I even ignore the fact that I haven't been able to spend time with my ownself for the past nine years!

"Why did you say *no* to your wife? Dude, go out, have fun! That's how you kill your boredom! And just now you said you need a break, right?" Ninad sounds genuinely concerned… "It really pinches me dude, when guys like you crib in life! *Arrey*, you guys've got everything but still… I really don't understand…."

Do I really need to tell Ninad what am I going through? May be no. But thanks Ninad; you have definitely set the ball rolling… Your perplexing thoughts have somehow been compelling me to realise that it's time to get over this frustrating flatness! May be, I should quit my job! So many people do that… . These days nobody cares… . And tell me, what's wrong in changing jobs? I think I have anyway contributed enough to this company… and seven and half years is not a joke! I agree that I am being paid pretty well but I am sure others will pay even better!

I am sure a change of jobs will put me back into my real self! People do need change in their lives and so do I. I know it's a late realisation but I guess I'm finally making the right move….

It was getting late in the office but the thought of quitting my job kept me in good spirits! I spent the entire afternoon working on my resume.

"Beep… Beep…" I was lost… The phone kept ringing.

"Dude, your wife had called on my mobile phone. What happened? You guys had a fight?"

I barely had intentions to clarify and just responded to Ninad with a vague smile. Promptly, he made some mischievous assumptions, which I could read in his twinkling eyes, and he went out of the cabin nodding and whistling….

Apu would be late tonight. Her reviews with the Board are normally quite elaborate… I wish she could come a little early today… I desperately need to speak to her about my decision….

Ting Tong… "Honey, how much time would you take to open the door? You just do this everyday… I really don't like this!" Apu is back. "The review went on till 10.30, so we ordered some pizzas. Why didn't you go out with Shiv for dinner? That poor guy must have called you a thousand times…." She would go on; probably she couldn't hear me saying that Shiv and I have just been back from *Delight* – our good old beer joint at M.G. Road!

Apu looks apparently dozy and I know that nothing on this earth can now stop her from asking me to just get lost! She does that often when I don't let her sleep... and impose my brainless childhood anecdotes at one o'clock in the night! But tonight, it's my future's turn....

Apu has never been too keen about my times of yore but I guess she wouldn't be so indifferent if I talk about my, I mean, *our* future....

"Sid, how can you even think of quitting your job? Have you ever imagined in the wildest of your dreams what it could mean to us...? How the hell you think we would even manage our medical expenses? How will we ever be able to have our own child? Besides, it has been almost eight years for you now, right? You think you would be able to adjust anywhere else? And tell me honestly, what is it that you are looking for in your new job? You are being paid so well, you get respect in your company, and you enjoy great relationships.... Are you still disturbed about the Sydney affair? Why can't you just forget things and concentrate on...." She can't go beyond... rather she won't, because it's she who has been really disturbed about the 'Sydney affair'!

I just wondered if I would ever be able to make my wife understand what I really had to say. But I understood it for sure that I must do something about the way I am dealing with my life. I have understood that my job of late has been a real depressant. So quitting it is inevitable. But Apu's right – I must introspect. What is it that I didn't like here? What would have kept me happy? Where did things go wrong? I must find answers to these questions before I genuinely decide to quit! So as Apu persists, it has to be a conscious, well-informed decision!

"Honey, please don't do this to yourself ! Come, at least sleep well tonight...." Apu insists but no, I can't let these thoughts fade into the dark again. I think I should take a day's off tomorrow and spend some quality time digging further....

"Honey...!!!"

I know I won't get even a blink of sleep but at times it feels good to listen to your wife! I lie down next to her with my eyes wide open struggling between untamed thoughts and an unfamiliar bewilderment….

"Sid, aren't you going to office today?"

My fault… I should have told Apu.

"Are you crazy? We have to save our leaves for October…. How else do you think are we going to Turkey for our anniversary? You are sick! …Whatever…!!! I am going… I can't be an escapist as you!"

You wouldn't believe this but for the first time ever in the last seven and half years I have decided to take a day's off for no *precise* reason. Well, I do go on leave; but only on genuine grounds. But today, I decided not to go to work just to figure out the reason why I felt the need to do so! I think the urge to discover the root of my crisis is getting grave… Oh, did I say *crisis*? Hmmm… I think it spells sense… Well, I can't scream eureka for sure but it seems I am somewhere close to it!

It's probably too early to make a statement; but I suspect that I am in the midst of a crisis. Is it what people call *midlife-crisis*?

I do remember reading about it in some lifestyle magazines. I have heard my knowledgeable friends often commenting on it with lot of concern and eagerness. I have also seen the weekend supplements of popular newspapers and tabloids carrying fancy features about it.

"I don't know if it's indeed a case of midlife crisis…." Wow, for a change, Ninad sounds credibly serious on the phone today!

I would agree with Ninad that it might not essentially be a case of midlife crisis… But with symptoms that evidently indicate signs of persistent turbulence at this juncture of my life, why shouldn't I take the elitist privilege of calling myself a victim of *midlife-crisis*!

Sounds satirical but in some dormant corner of my heart I was seriously excited and curious about this strange phenomenon!

Definitely, I need to dig it deeper now…and as Apu says, I must introspect… I must start doing it here and now!

I am getting desperate. I am trying hard to think, question and understand…. I am making assumptions with the hope that they might lead me to conclusions, though truth still eludes… I think I should just lie down for a while, listen to some music and come back fresh.

I pick up the photo album lying on the bookshelf next to my bed and stretch myself on the floor leaning against my couch. I feel a little composed… I hazily look at some of my old pictures from my Business School days…. And even before I ask myself a thing, my mind starts conjuring up… "Siddhartha, from what you tell me, I don't suppose, you are doing what you are actually capable of !" I suddenly remember the words of Dr. Varghese, who taught us Marketing Research. Couple of years back we had met at an alumni gathering and on being briefed about my job, he couldn't help saying so. "You were certainly not a mediocre student! You were so good Siddhartha!" Dr. Varghese's remarks did sound blunt…. Considering that I was better off than most of my batch-mates at that point of time, my ears weren't probably tuned to any comment of that sort.

But Dr. Varghese was right. I was not mediocre. Although, I had assumed that the statement he made was by and large from an academic perspective, it has just started making sense to me in the current context. Today, what I suffer from is not lack of riches or the regret over not being materially successful. It is not even the grief of losing a legacy to an uncle or a cousin. Nor is it the frustration of not being promoted or rewarded at work. I have been pretty lucky on all these counts….

A careful recollection of Dr. Varghese's words leads me to think that what I suffer from is the fact that what I am doing today is exactly what a billion others in the world do! Big deal?? Yes, it is a big deal! My father used to tell me often, "Never jump for the moon. You will just fall flat on your face. Always be aware of your limits and circumstances. Not everyone in this world has the luxury to dream...." And in spite of being warned repeatedly by my Dad, ever since my childhood I remained a staunch dreamer, unbelievably vague and indifferent about my material aspirations. Many a times, I did manage to hook things, which might have sounded like achievements to many. But what I really never wanted to become in life was a 'me-too'. I just hated being lost in the crowd. As a kid I used to spend considerable amount of time exploring what different could I do in life. But gradually, the *responsibility* that comes with the phenomenon of growing older pushed me into the habit of compromising.... A small but immediate gain started appearing far more attractive than the bigger but the distant ones. And that was the point... of my tryst with mediocrity!

The mediocrity that has discreetly victimised me is not academic or intellectual – it is more of an attitudinal phenomenon – a gradual transition into a perpetual state of mind, where man ceases to aspire and achieve. It is the tendency to do what million others are doing. It is the consent to settle down for anything less than what one truly deserves! This reminds me of my friend Riz's rather loud declaration on being knocked down once by eleven mugs of some horrendously stirring home made rice-beer. "Man becomes big with a big dream and a big resolve to realize it. And to be there one must dare to boldly defy all conventional standards!"

I don't dither to acknowledge that Dr. Varghese's abhorrent comments had left me pondering about my very existence but the demands of the material world were so compelling that I succumbed without even paying any significant thought to his sharp indications.... Though I was very much aware that the truth about mediocrity was never a completely alien concept to my own perceptive self, of late, the idea of pushing myself defiantly out of my comfort zone and venturing out into an entirely anonymous world discouraged my temptations... I felt bound by my duties to earn and by my greed to earn more... I wanted wealth, I longed for material success, I wanted to be better off...

with little or no extra effort. And today, if I put a few of my experiences together, I conclude that the degree of success can certainly not be measured in terms of how many dollars you generate every hour. It is rather what you do and how good you are at it! And most decisively – the kind of happiness that you derive out of it! Unfortunately, in my case, that happiness is absolutely missing…!

"Job satisfaction can never be hundred percent!" Apu loves to make this statement whenever she finds me cribbing about my job. "Honey, the grass is always greener on the side of the fence. Where else would you get the kind of luxuries you enjoy here?" She usually comments. But is the purpose of life all about being comfortable and enjoying luxuries? In the past couple of years, I have done almost everything to keep my materialistic-self pampered. I bought the most expensive car that I could afford, moved into a bigger house and went to the most exotic places in the world for vacations. But there is no end to it. The more I did, the more I craved for! This is precisely where people like me fall into the trap! That's where mediocrity becomes your way of life…

Gosh… it's one o'clock. Now, who's going to cook lunch! Let me order some good Biryani from Fakhrooz. God! Can't tell you how much I love this Biryani!

Ting Tong… There comes my Biryani!

Ummm… Amazing!! As I unpack my Biryani, I realise that it has indeed been a great day – my self-confessions are leading to revelations quite beyond my expectations… I am sure the Biryani would taste even better today…

No! It tastes just the same… as great and special as ever…

People just fail to believe how Fakhrooz makes its Biryani taste so elegant and different! It's something that even the best of the breed Mughlai restaurants fail to deliver! Apu feels there's no secret. "It just happens to be the best." But I have always felt that Fakhrooz's secret has been in its brave decision to make its Biryani taste significantly different from the conventional preparation and yet maintain the superlative gastronomic standards over and over again.

I remember Mohammad Anees, the owner of Fakhrooz, once telling me, "*Arrey Bhaijaan*, cooking Biryani was my favourite pastime in my younger days, you know? My father was an Imam and wanted me to become a lawyer. I did go to college but couldn't complete my graduation. I lost my father and my maternal uncle took over his position. I left home in search of a job and weeks later I joined a small transport company in Bulandshahar as an office assistant. *Allah*! I was such a disaster… Soon I was chucked off from that job for not too surprising reasons. And after that I changed seven jobs without sticking to any beyond three months. I knew it was enough! But hardly did I know what I could take up next. I had a cousin in Mumbai who worked for a caterer and I decided to join him. I came to Mumbai and worked with him for a year. He knew that I was a little educated and hence tried persuading me to learn some English and try for a waiter's job in any of those upmarket South Mumbai restaurants. I did give it a shot but it never came *instinctively*… I was disappointed and desperately wanted to know what my instincts could do for me! I realised that the only instinctive skill that I could turn to for my survival was cooking Biryani. But you know *Bhaijaan*, we are from the North and people in Mumbai and Pune don't have the taste for Awadhi food, so I decided to create a fusion style of cooking. I started my own catering service and four years later I bought this shop and named it Fakhrooz after my late father. *Khuda ke karam se*, everything's fit and fine today. Anees, who was kicked out of every job that he did, today stands as the proud owner of *Fakhrooz* – the synonym of Biryani for millions across western India! And *inshallah*, this year *Bhaijaan* I am sending both my sons to Switzerland for their postgraduation in Hospitality Management! *Kasam se Bhaijaan*, the only thing that I have learnt over these years is the power of your *junoon*, your passion! You should never think twice to follow your passion, that's the path Allah Himself has chosen for you."

Good food… good food for thought… But it's actually strange that having known Anees *bhai* and his story for so many years, I could never gauge the extent of similarities between us! If I think more about it, I am also compelled to look at the divergence and I realise that it could have been awfully easy for Anees *bhai* to get into the grip of mediocrity and remain a not-so-good waiter in a not-too-bad restaurant for his lifetime. Like me, he too could have saved his job for ten or more years. He too could have compromised… But he dared….

Beep…beep. Beep…beep. "Honey, I am reaching home at five thirty. Is that fine? I mean, are you done with your stuff ?" And before I could answer, Apu continued, "So now, can you tell me why we hate Mondays?"

The answer was yes but I didn't want to elaborate on the phone. I just told her that it has been so because each Monday came as an unconscious reminder of the *vicious cycle of mediocrity* that drifted us doggedly from our instincts and passions and pushed us further deep into a state of aimlessness and despair. Apu was stunned! "And you realised this today?" she questioned in all innocence and surprise.

I would agree with Apu; I actually realised it today… wow, what a thing is human mind! It just requires a perfect masturbation and thoughts lying deep down ejaculate unstoppably! I am just astonished at the way the mystic human genius connects discrete dormant thoughts and heaves strings of incredible revelations. Good Lord! Things that were entrenched in my mind since ages didn't even occur to me all this while… True, it just requires a perfect masturbation!

2

A Life of Purpose and Passion

FEEBLY warm, dry windy evenings... It's springtime in Pune. Undoubtedly, there's something extraordinarily special about these evenings that has mesmerised me every time spring has dawned in this city in the past fifteen years.

"But things are changing... Pune is gradually losing its old charm!" I get to hear this rather recurrently from most of the old-timers in the city. Painful...! Having spent almost a half of my life here, I have been a witness to the colossal cultural shift that Pune has undergone over these years of *remarkable change*. From the unobtrusively quiet *Oxford of the East* to the bustling IT mega-city, I have seen Pune changing its face every passing day. Honestly, now at times I feel like a stranger here....

Disturbing thoughts... They often leave me dead....

Dead on my feet, I walk up to my bedroom windows; pull off the curtains and watch the sun setting in the dusty western skies....

Strains of fond and foul memories flash before my eyes as they stretch beyond the windows to catch a glimpse of the tired day quietly slithering into the fading vermilion....

Ting Tong... That must be Apu!

"Honey...Guess what? I have got movie-tickets for the International Film Festival that's going on at the National Film

Archives! Cool, *na*? And we are going on the third day when they are screening Iranian and Russian films only!" Apu looks in high spirits!

"I know honey, you had been pretty disturbed since yesterday about your job; so I thought let's do something interesting!"

God! Apu thinks that I am disturbed? Well, she has every right to believe so! But that's not the truth and, I want her to understand that I am not disturbed… I am just exploring! In fact I want her to appreciate that I am not up to any brainless act of escapism! Neither am I getting driven for a surrender of any sort! I want her to understand that I still want to fight and win. And to make that happen, I must find my way....

I don't intend to recoil from my responsibilities and seek refuge at an ascetic abode! I am not even trying to ignore my material well-being either! No! In fact, it's absolutely the other way round… Now I want more from life! I want to be really alive! I want to be really happy! I desperately want to be excited about things that I do and for this to happen I must do things that come instinctively to me – things where I see a purpose, things that I am truly passionate about! I am sure, with this milieu, Apu wouldn't have a reason to resist…. But I am sure she would turn precariously wild if I tell her that I am yet to figure out what my purpose and passion could possibly be!

"Look Sid, I really don't care what you do in life! I know it for sure that whatever you do you would do it reasonably well. But what I can't appreciate is this frivolous attitude of yours. Why can't you just accept things as they are and try to get your best bargain out of them? You don't have to tell me right now but just ask yourself what is it that you think you are genuinely passionate about! I know that you are good at too many things…. You can cook, you can sing, you can repair the car and you can make wonderful cocktails… but tell me, can you really think of making a successful or for that matter even a career out of these?" Apu makes her point pretty clear. She bluntly points out that my introspection was still far from being complete!

Now the million dollar question for me is – What is my passion? What is my purpose? What am I really good at? And the further I think about it, I get all the more confused....

May be I should I ask myself if I have ever been good at anything....

Apu's busy this evening with some Lebanese lamb preparation. Wow! It smells delicious... I must admit, Apu's cooking skills have definitely matured over the past couple of years....

Well, with Apu in the kitchen and the spring blushing at its peak, the only thing that I feel goes best with the calm evening breeze is a few mugs of chilled beer at my balcony... And yes, a yet another spirited round of cerebral masturbation....

Beep...beep. Beep...beep. "*Oye* Sid, have you guys booked your tickets? Listen; come before April ends, okay? You know how the summer is over here!" My best pal, Major Riz Khan has been insisting for long on a trip to Shimla. Actually, he is on a *peace posting* in Delhi since the last year and it has been a while that we four, I mean, I and Apu, and Riz and his wife Leena have gone on a vacation together. "Just get them booked *yaar*! Tell me, where's the confusion? You know it *bugger*, I don't like this fussiness!"

We have been planning this trip for quite a while and Riz knows that even this time I would finally back out! "Then what's the point in discussing... I'll talk to Aparoopa. You'll move only when she kicks your ass...." He was irritated. I pleaded not to hang up. In fact, I was happy that he called at the right time....

I hurriedly told him about my newly discovered experience of cerebral masturbation.... He giggled and calmed down.

I asked Riz if he has ever found me genuinely passionate about anything... something that comes instinctively to me. He sounded puzzled... and astonished. He said he was stunned that we all believe that we know our people to their core, but almost every time it is just a belief ! "Leave aside your people; we in actual fact don't even know our own selves... Sad indeed...." Amazed and disillusioned, Riz concluded, "The quest for the world of knowledge begins and ends at self-exploration"!

Riz also made an interesting point.... He asked me if Apu has ever found me too excited about anything in life in the past ten years. Sounds interesting! Let me ask Apu....

Apu is setting the dining table. Hmmm... Fairly tempting... The lamb looks great!

"Sid, it took me three hours! I hope it tastes good."

Apu's trying to avoid my question... I repeat it: Has there been a day in your life when you have found me sufficiently excited about my job or anything else for that matter?

"Sid I need some time to think. Even otherwise, I think we should sleep early tonight. You haven't been sleeping well for the past few nights."

I quietly finished my dinner and slipped into the bedroom hoping that I'll get up early in the morning and try talking to Apu.

"Get up quickly, Sid. Let's go out to the lawn for a walk. You wanted to talk to me, right?" Oh Apu, you are such a darling! I am sure; I couldn't have found a better wife on this earth!

"Well Sid, I honestly think that you have never been excited about anything at work. Yes, when your team goes on an outing, you are a different man altogether. You talk so much, you amuse everyone; in fact, you enliven the whole experience of the outing. But the next morning, the same man just refuses to smile! You look dull, irritated and lost! Tell me Sid, what do I conclude?"

I moaned at Apu's rather thoughtful observation as she continued, "I have found you extremely intelligent when it comes to personal finances, investments, purchases... everything! In fact, I have always admired you for your clarity and decisiveness. You are always so firm on your domestic and personal matters! But whenever I have seen you talking about work, you look terrible, you sound irritated, I mean, you are just not yourself! What makes you so uncomfortable, Sid? You have been pretty successful in your career. You are so good. You have been recognised sufficiently.

Then what keeps you so overwrought over your job? Why is it that most of your colleagues of late have started finding you reserved and aloof?"

"Sid, I have seen this time and again that you are very happy when you are yourself ! And you are yourself when you do things that you really enjoy doing. Perhaps I have told this to you even before but I genuinely believe that you can do well in whatever you take up. But, Sid, whenever you think of taking up a new career, please do ensure that it allows you to be your real self.... Well, I personally feel that you have got extremely good writing skills. And I very well remember that in our college days you really enjoyed writing.... If you ask me, I would suggest you try your luck in writing... Who knows, it might turn out a fortune for you... well, it's just a suggestion; you may look at other alternatives like music and cookery as well! So, you please carry on with your quest...."

Apu surprised me again. This time all the more with her *power breakfast*!

Beep...beep. "Hey Siddhartha...! This is Kalra from Tokyo. How are you doing, my man? Heard from Ninad that you haven't been keeping well.... What happened? Told you so many times, you must exercise. You can't imagine the kind of difference forty-five minutes of Yoga every day can make to your life. Try it! You are so young. At your age, I didn't even know how it feels to fall sick! By the way, what's the problem? ...Go to the doctor if required.... Rest well. Take more leaves if you want. I want to see you fit and fine when I reach Pune this Friday."

Kalra said it. And I quietly agreed that I would need a few more days of rest. Apu doesn't have to worry much about my leaves; Kalra has assured that he would recommend HR to treat this entire week's off as specially sanctioned paid sick leaves. Indeed... at times the world really looks perfect!

"Honey, was that Kalra? Seems he has asked you to rest, right? And what will happen to your leaves? How will we go to Turkey? But who cares? You just sit here and meditate or do whatever you want! How does it affect you whether or not I get to celebrate my wedding anniversary? Too selfish you are, Sid!"

God, it's really a struggle to get Apu let you explain... and finally... "What? You mean you've got an entire week's holiday with pay?" She is pleasantly surprised.

"Great, Mr. Kumar! Have a great time! I guess a week is long enough time for you to accomplish your grand quest. All the best...!" Apu sounds a little sarcastic but I know she'll be fine....

I really don't know if the week would be good enough to accomplish my quest. I don't know if it would be enough to re-discover my estranged reveries and relive the ones that I still might feel passionate and instinctive about. I don't even know if these five days would let me understand how courageous and liberated I feel about reliving my reveries? But what I precisely know is that in these five days I can very well take the quest further – unfolding pages from my past and re-discovering yet another facet of mine every day....

"Hello Sid, are you still on...? ...But mind you, the very idea of a quest is too massively romantic... And knowing you, I am pretty sure that it will push you to flow with your tendency of going on and on!"

I agree with Apu but at the moment, my desperate crave for a rendezvous with my long lost reveries is no less romantic either...

An hour of overriding thoughts in deep reclusion passed by in absolute silence and I decided to pamper myself with a mug of fresh ground coffee.

I was wondering why suddenly Apu asked me to try my luck in writing...! Was I really so passionate a writer ever?

Lost in these thoughts, I closed my eyes and dived deep into my past, voyaged across lands and ages to fetch a bunch of words that I had written years ago on a ratty old piece of paper and had dumped it into some dark corner of one of the vintage cupboards at my ancestral home. It read, *"I aspire to nurture soothing reveries for the weary eyes. I endeavour to instil a divine elation into deprived souls. I dream to celebrate life with the innocent joys of the ever exuberant child in me!"*

Sounds interesting and surprisingly relevant... There is purpose. There is passion... but I doubt if I correctly remember the context? I think I do... Yes... I do! These were the lines from an English play that our group was rehearsing for our school's annual day celebrations. I was playing the lead role of Raphael, the young poet and playwright who in spite of being the only child of a Lord discards his father's riches to build his own intellectual wealth on the merit of his literary talent. I was barely thirteen and the play with its *avant-garde* spirit and emphatic dialogues had left an enduring impression.

Ten rounds of vigorous rehearsal sessions had left everyone in the group desiring to grow up into a Raphael, *aspiring to nurture tender dreams for the weary eyes and instil divine elation into deprived souls* !

True; playing Raphael was an experience beyond expression.... For months together it was just impossible to alienate myself from the clout of Raphael. As a matter of fact, till couple of years from then, that was the only name that many in the school knew me by.

The entire feel of being Raphael had such an astounding effect on my adolescent self that it inspired me immensely to seek creative pleasures and create dreams for the world that uphold hope, love and life!

Gradually, the influence of Raphael grew beyond... The quest went a far of books, poetry and music.... Those were the days when I experienced the allure of love for the first ever time in my life... in the *celebrated* love story of Rituraj and Anamika.

Rituraj was one of the thirty odd post graduate students of English literature in the local government college. His poems, often seen in the neighbourhood vernacular publications, were an object of discussion and praise among the young artistic lot in the town.

My first rendezvous with Rituraj was incidentally just a coincidence. It all started with a mistaken knock at the door of my house expecting Anamika, my next-door neighbour's daughter to open it. Funnily, when I had opened the door, Rituraj, the person who was knocking the door, wasn't at all surprised to see me! "Call your sister, please" ...and I had to question him back to know the name of my sister, as I didn't have any! And that was the beginning of a friendship with a man to whom all that mattered in life was to love and being loved.

Rituraj was an amateur percussionist and had accompanied Anamika, a reasonably well-trained vocalist, at a few local concerts here and there. Artistes in love! That's precisely the reason why I developed a strange sort of affinity for them. To me, they were Raphael's folks – God's chosen ones for *nurturing tender dreams for the weary eyes and instilling divine elation into deprived souls*!

In the company of Rituraj and Anamika, I started growing up almost detached from the world around, passionately looking forward to enthrall my fellow *Raphaelists* with my lyrical ballads that narrated sagas of immortal love and boundless optimism. Right out of the blue, life had started to seem so beautiful....

And then, amidst our pristine world, around the serene confluence of art and love, raised a tornado that shattered our tranquil abode of dreams... *The fall of the great Raphaelean era*!

It was drizzling since morning.... The monsoons that year had been retarded by almost a month. I was sitting alone at the outer veranda of our cottage, besieged with some odd verses in anticipation of the rains.... Suddenly, it thunders aloud and I lose my lines... Vaguely, I see Rituraj standing across the lane. He was all drenched... I walked up to him and he sighed, "It's all over Siddhartha! Anamika's father is adamant that she marries Chirantan; remember that idiot with those funny specs? That *bastard* is now a Nuclear Physicist in Delhi! He is leaving for the US this year for his post-doctorate research, damn it!"

"This was bound to happen! Anamika is one of the prettiest girls in the community. She definitely deserves a well established groom. Girls like her are not meant for petty clerical jobs in rickety old government offices. They are born with the fortune of *maharanis*! You think she would be happy marrying a vagabond who can't even afford a decent living for himself ! Artiste, huh! I have seen enough of these clowns in my life! *Bloody scoundrel*...."

Anamika's father was a simple old man. Having retired as a Head Clerk from one of those *rickety old government offices*, he always dreamt of marrying off his only child to a highly educated, affluent US-based groom… Chirantan, though comes from a very modest family, has today *uplifted* himself to the status of an internationally-famed scientist. In fact, this is the best possible blend Anamika's father could ever expect—a US-based groom with *strong Indian roots*!

"I won't give up Siddhartha! Life is all about love and understanding… I am more than confident that Anamika and I can make a much better future together. It's not just about living abroad and making big bucks! What do you think that Chirantan is up to? He just needs a maid in the US! Just tell me Siddhartha, can I let my love become somebody else's object of pity or torture! If her father wants me to take up a job, I will do so. If he wants me to go abroad, I promise I will give it my best shot! But even the thought of letting Anamika go is killing. I can't bear it Siddhartha… It's really killing… Tell her Siddhartha, she is killing me...."

It was impossible watching my living Raphael yelling insanely at the mercilessness of the cruel world. Alas! I was just too young and helpless to do a thing and that was making me feel all the more miserable….

Anamika's family was busy preparing for the ring ceremony…. In fact, the wedding wouldn't have been too far… But Chirantan's father, just a week before, while on his regular morning walk slipped off the stairs of a nearby park and died on the spot following a serious brain haemorrhage. The wedding had to be postponed by a year's time. Days passed… the couple got engaged and Chirantan left for the US, leaving Anamika wavering between her dwindling past and an uncertain future….

Rituraj was still hopeful. He moved to Delhi and took up a job… 'Documentation Specialist' at a Research Agency... "Hello Siddhartha?" He would often call me in the evenings. "Tell Anamika's father that within the next two years I will surpass Chirantan in every possible way. Tell him that he can always evade the guilt, which he might otherwise have to suffer from in the future. There's still time.... It has just been three months and my company's already considering me for a Research Analyst's position! Who knows tomorrow even I might land up in the US? Tell me Siddhartha, whom will I blame if this really happens?"

Weeks passed and so did months... . The undying dilemma of choosing between the love of her life and the supposed sumptuousness of the world unseen was deviously grabbing Anamika's obsession.... Often tempted by the subtle desire of chasing the possibilities, and often, carried away by the fond memories of the times spent with Rituraj, Anamika fought her conscience everyday to finally gather the guts and make the unpleasant utterances....

"Rituraj, I am not too unhappy about the way things have shaped up for us. I think this is what is called destiny.... Seems really strange but isn't it true that only a couple of months back all that mattered to us in life was just being together? But did we ever ask ourselves why we really wanted so? Did we even bother to gauge the amount of harm we were doing to ourselves in the guise of being together? Rituraj, we have always been honest to each other and for the sake of this honesty, I want to tell you something.... For someone like me who on her own cannot afford the kind of life I am heading for, it matters a lot to hook on to the right opportunities at the right time! After all, in this world of vanity and conceit, where do you think you and I together could have stood with our humble background and a meek tomorrow? Rituraj, I can't express how I wish that you were Chirantan.... Life could have been so beautiful.... But never mind! I am optimistic as ever.... There must be a purpose behind this act of destiny. In fact, I can already see the change.... Just keep your spirits high, do well and never look back...."

"How can she do this to me? Believe me, so often in the past I had seen her ridiculing Chirantan for his girly pink shirts and the huge funny spectacles! You know, he happened to be six years older to us, but still he never had the guts even to make an eye contact with us…I have heard from my cousins when he was in the University, even the most idiotic creature there called him *chimpu* for his chimpanzee-like looks!"

Rituraj's calls to me became all the more frequent as the wedding date drew closer. It was his sheer optimism that he still believed things could turn to his favour.

One evening, he called up again. This time he seemed a little composed…. He said he wanted to speak to Anamika… and, they spoke… though not for too long… within moments Anamika hanged up the phone and left without saying a word to me. I wasn't surprised. I could sense what the conversation must have been about... Unquestionably, a sad parting note; what else!

I was wrong! And I realised this the next morning when Rituraj called up again. He had some good news to share. He didn't elaborate but wanted me to know that I need not be worried and he would never let me down! "Siddhartha, your Raphael won't fall!" He was confident and sounded genuinely happy!

A week later, with merely four more days to go for the wedding, Rituraj rings my door-bell on an early Sunday morning… cheery, relaxed and firm! I wasn't really surprised but couldn't weigh the possibilities either….

"Guess Siddhartha, what all must have I done that you see me here today, all set to steal my girl from the world? And why 'steal'? I will rightfully seek her hand from her father and fly her away with me to Singapore!"

Singapore?

"Yes. Singapore! …Now don't ask me why Singapore… It just happened… but honestly, I am quite happy about it! I think, by and large what has become the most common yardstick of an average Indian's success or failure in life is the distance he travels away from India to earn his bread! You are called a worthless *swine* who's worthy of nothing if you *shamelessly* live and work in your own country. Fortunately, I am not one of them anymore…."

Rituraj sounded very different. No doubts, I was happy for him but somewhere I missed his old charm and simplicity.

"You know that in Delhi I was working for a Research Agency, right? ...In fact, it all started there... I was put on a critical project for a Singapore-based client and since the past three months I was asked to manage it single-handedly. The project went off pretty well and the client grew immensely appreciative about my work! The head of our company's Singapore subsidiary, who is also the Account Manager for this client, called me up and offered me to join the Singapore operations with *immediate effect*! ...So how does it sound, little Raphael?"

I was amazed! Actually, I could have never imagined Rituraj, the small town romantic poet and musician, going all the way to a place like Singapore and managing the show on his own for a multinational firm... I kept nodding, generally wondered at life for unveiling endless surprises....

"Siddhartha, I am surprised that you didn't ask me a thing about Chirantan... I know you must have thought it will hurt me, right? Probably yes; if I hadn't spoken to him before coming here, I too would have hated discussing him! Yes, I spoke to him yesterday over phone. Well Siddhartha, you won't believe, he turned out to be such a wonderful gentleman! He's indeed a gem. ...When I told him how hard I have struggled in the past eleven months to win Anamika and her father's esteem and appreciation, he couldn't help himself from breaking into a weepy sigh! He promised all support and said that he himself will talk to Anamika's father and convince him...."

"Oh Siddhartha... What a thing success is! Success... sweet success! Just look at me; don't you see the magic it has worked? Trust me, it's just phenomenal.... It feels so good... Siddhartha, I want even you to experience it! You know Siddhartha, you are almost half my age, but genuinely you have been the most reliable friend all along... I wish I could share my success with you.... Nevertheless, let me at the least share some secrets that I have discovered about success! ...I am saying this because sadly I am seeing a Rituraj of yesterdays bit by bit creeping into you everyday.... For God's sake, stay away from him! How much ever tempted you are, never ever fall a prey to the weird illusions of his vagabondism, which he artfully manages to mask under his artistic aspirations! Always be practical and stay committed to your acquisitive self! You grow as your appetite grows, mind it!"

I kept ogling and listening as Rituraj went on talking about his post marriage plans, career opportunities, and quality of life in Singapore.... Neither of us did realise that these could probably be our last and ultimate times spent together....

I went on listening but Rituraj's words of acute disregard and detestation for the values that he once religiously endorsed obliged me to quietly grin at the irony of life! And as I thought along I felt an unusual sense of vulnerability... I found myself completely lost amongst the putrid words of curtailed poetry.... It was an agonising experience... and my little pubescent soul found it all the more difficult to stand the throbbing of seeing my Raphael falling apart—the artiste consciously succumbing to the insensitive demands of the distressed lover!

Anamika was right; this is what is called destiny!

3

Lost Focus

"HONEY...! Come on, get up now.... It has been four days and you haven't even stepped out of the house. Trust me; it's too bad for your health! Come; let's go for a walk...."

In our college days, Aparoopa and I often used to go on long strolls in the evenings. The obnoxiously jam-packed Fergusson College Road of today and some of its equally crowded by-lanes in those times were far quieter but no less colourful a stretch for a wholesome evening walk.... Probably that's precisely why both of us still find those strolls far more than mere good times spent together. In fact, most of the crucial decisions of our life, including that of our marriage, were made during some of those memorable strolls....

Even today, I just love it when Apu asks me for a stroll! May be, it's just another expression of her reassurance that she still cares....

"So Mr. Kumar, you have been pretty hushed these days.... What happened? What have you been thinking about?" Apu was doing her routine check....

I thought for a while and wondered where to begin... There was so much that I wanted to tell her! But finally, what I ended up expressing must had come to her as some sort of a stupid riddle and I was sure that she didn't even bother to think about it.

I told her how the life of passion which I had experienced once in my childhood was devastated in the streets of Doom Dooma and how mediocrity in the guise of challenges deceptively crept into my juvenile psyche.

Apu was smiling and nodding in agreement. I was wrong again!

"So it seems you are almost there. What is it then? Have you been able to figure out?" The probing goes on.

Yes, I am there. I am almost there at Doom Dooma....

Rituraj and Anamika's dramatic wedding and their immediate departure had left me in a dire state of gloom and seclusion. More than the stale aftertaste of Rituraj's hypocrisy and obscured vulnerability, being practically left without a friend in that suffocating locale was disconcerting... and with the patrons of my youthful reveries diverging away to seek the end of their newfound dreams, the gradual yet premature death of the passionate poet in me seemed inevitable....

Almost around the same time, 'Doom Dooma' happened... In fact, at that point of time, I couldn't have wished for a better timing for my father's transfer!

I was fifteen and had just been promoted to the Tenth standard. But my lame dreams and shaken values had turned me terribly indifferent and aimless for a person of my age. Unlike others who shared benches with me in the school, I simply failed to cultivate the aspiration of going to a college that taught medicine, business or technology. Honestly, I didn't even ever bother to ponder on how I would earn my bread when I grow up! I was not pessimistic.... It was just that things didn't matter and I loved being lost and left to myself.

Interestingly, when nothing in the world seemed fascinating enough to catch my fancy, I began to relish the small little joys in the apparently indolent yet lively town of Doom Dooma.

It was the peak of summer and in one of those moist warm mornings as I packed my bag for my first day in the new school, I felt the sunny joy of a new day... It was a new beginning indeed....

The school in Doom Dooma that I had joined was one of its kinds in many aspects. It was a public school hosted exactly in the middle of a paramilitary base with over ten barracks right inside the school premises. The approach to the school was through a shabby motor workshop where night patrol vans were repaired and serviced. The most interesting experience one could expect however was entering the nicely decorated office of the principal and speaking to the young teacher in his mid-twenties sitting there with an air of authority, subtly explicating that the school had been without a principal for past several years.

"Oh yes Mr. Kumar, please come in." The principal in-charge, Mr. Arun Pratap Singh, stood up to shake hands with my father. "You know Mr. Kumar, ours is not a very big school. We have just around 400 students. But we are doing really well. Today, except for Mathematics, we have the entire Secondary School faculty in place." Seeing my father's absolute inability to hide his evident disappointment, Mr. Singh immediately added with an appeasing smile, "The Mathematics teacher is also expected soon."

Mr. Singh called for an office peon who languidly led me to my classroom.

The classroom was all empty. There was no one to be seen except for a girl who cared the least to take her eyes off the book she was mutely reading. We didn't speak. I turned my head and my rolling eyes hit the blackboard and I noticed 'Games' written on it. I took a seat in the front row and dropped my bag off. After spending a few minutes gazing across the handmade charts and collages stuck on the walls, I took out a book and started browsing it casually.... Suddenly, I hear the loud noise of a group rushing in.

"Who's he?" Somebody screamed. "Must be Maya's boy-friend...Hahahahaha... Can't you see the book in his hand? Bloody bookworm...."

I had always heard and read that the "first impression is the last impression." But I, on the contrary, had repeatedly experienced that the first impression at almost all times came with a certain degree of falsity and fallacy. However, in my case, though started off with a loose comment, the impression of being a bookworm persisted across years of my association with my fellows from Doom Dooma!

I was amazed… rather excited about my new-found identity and soon I saw myself spending long hours at the study table solving mathematical problems and preparing notes. My teachers were impressed and a few almost laid a bet on me as the most probable topper of the batch in the Secondary School Exams. This was a new experience. *Being studious* was probably the least of the things that I could have ever been consciously serious about…. Nevertheless, I was just surprised by the upshot of a casual comment….

At the crossroads of this eventful transition I made friends with a few of my classmates, which added to the excitement that Doom Dooma had brought into my life. Mridul, Debo, Pranit, Dhanjit and Abhilekh… Wow! I was not a loner anymore….

Small little things like cycling all the way to the riverside to watch the summer sun setting, climbing the hillock behind the Shiva Temple to fly our hand-made gliders, befriending the *chaatwallah* for petty discounts and spending hours at the petite book stalls to pick the right and the cheapest ones; every experience seemed too uplifting…. The captivating sight of the crowning greenery, the glittering golden drops of the summer sun, the narrow serpentine lanes of tar vanishing into nowhere.... I was really moved by the stunning splendour of simplicity! And thus, life rolled on with the joyful wheels of our bicycles, rummaging around for the unknown treasures….

"Wow honey! That sounds so good! So refreshing! Well that reminds me; let me get some nice fresh coffee for you. By the way, where are you now in your quest? Did Doom Dooma prove to be of any help?"

Contrary to my apprehensions, Doom Dooma, in actual fact, further fanned the poetic fire in me. I was helplessly pushed by some unknown force within me to pick up the pen and scream out all my dormant feelings and desires on paper… I would have probably given up on everything and resorted to full-time poetry hadn't I fallen for the mystery called Maya!

"Congratulations Siddhartha! You have scored the highest marks in the First Term Exams. Hmmm…. You seem to be really good!"

God, I could have never imagined Maya, the girl who never spoke a word to anyone around, came and congratulated me. Maya had always been holding the first rank in the class and a few of us had mockingly named her 'The Unbeaten Champ'! A few others, mostly the females, called her 'bitch', though I could never ever even distantly relate her to one.

'The Champ is beaten' was the buzz, though I knew it for sure that it was I who was beaten by Maya's implausible warmth and compelling personality.

Soon, we started exchanging notes more often than before. We became what could plainly be seen as good friends. We saw ourselves spending more time knowing and understanding each other. To me, it was a new feeling, somewhat overwhelming, to see the other side of the tiny little quiet lady... I discovered that she was a powerhouse of talent. She was a trained classical dancer, a vocalist and a true enthusiast of English poetry and drama…. But unlike me, she seldom carried the attitude of being gifted.

Another thing that amusingly drew Maya and me closer was a common acquaintance, who was none other than Anamika. Small world…! Maya and Anamika were pen-pals who at all times remained in touch through letters. In fact, it was Maya from who I learnt of late that Rituraj and Anamika were in Delhi and if truth be told, they had been in Delhi ever since they got married! Maya also hinted that things weren't quite fine with them and Rituraj was almost certainly seeing someone else.

Maya called their marriage a disaster and eventually persuaded me to concur that it wasn't just enough to love and be loved.

This was just one instance but I had always sensed an apparent disillusionment in Maya's ideas about love and marriage. I had heard her saying this more than often that "Love is not real; it's an illusion or may be at the most a state of mind." And every time I heard her saying that I just used to wish that she could understand someday what it meant to live in that *state of mind*!

Well, being 'the only guy who Maya talks to' was a label. But to me, being close to someone like Maya was a privilege that not too many could ever expect! She was so different from the world. In fact, the more I learnt about her, the more I started revering her for what she was....

Maya was not born to a happy, conventionally married, socially accepted couple. Local gossips suggest that her father, George Thomas, a middle-aged Malayalee Christian, was a dentist at a local polyclinic, who was forcefully married to his seventeen-year-old nursing assistant, Indranee, for distinctively obvious reasons.... If rumours were to be believed, weeks following this star-crossed marriage, George had supposedly ended his life by consuming several bottles of rat-poison, leaving his pregnant wife Indranee all alone amidst the untold miseries of destiny. Months later, Maya was born to the ill-fated mother.

For Indranee, this was definitely not her first encounter with adversity. Orphaned at the age of six, this unfortunate daughter of a poor Brahmin, having being brought up at an orphanage supported by the local Brahmagyana Mission Hospital, was more than conscious of what it meant to stay alive and bring up her little one against the unending odds of fate. Though shattered to the core of her soul, she knew that she couldn't afford to sit back and mourn. And as they say, life must go on, with little Maya in her arms, Indranee went back to the Mission Hospital, sought the renowned philanthropist Swami Keshavananda's help and succeeded in availing a scholarship to pursue her pre-university education and thereafter a Bachelor's course in Nursing. By the time Indranee passed out of the Nursing College, Maya was almost four and had started going to the primary school run by the Mission.

Indranee got the job of a senior nurse at the maternity ward of the Mission Hospital and got herself increasingly involved in welfare activities in the locales of Doom Dooma. She continued working with the Mission till her massive popularity got her elected as the local Legislator from Doom Dooma a few years from then and she became the legendary Indranee Goswami!

"Siddhartha, I must tell you that you are blessed with an extraordinarily sharp intelligence.... Don't you think you should make the best out of it? Siddhartha, stop being a day dreamer! You are capable of greater actions and it would be great injustice if you waste your time and talent writing poetry and reading novels! Even I have an inclination for finer things in life. But I strongly believe that you shouldn't just do what you like, you should rather do what is right!"

Maya was getting more vocal about me. Perhaps, it was purely out of her genuine concern.... But what I always enjoyed was being told that I am important and I somehow started reciprocating her comments with gestures that could convince her that she was valued. In fact, she was genuinely valued!

Maya was certainly not one of those who could bowl you off in seconds.... No, she was not beautiful. At least not a startling beauty.... But to me, her looks never really mattered till one fine afternoon while coming back from the school, I finally slithered into the awe of insane adolescent infatuation....

It was a normal day... at least it did start like one... The blackberry trees at the backyard of the school looked no less inviting. The motor workshop behind the Physics laboratory was emanating its usual noise. Even the music teacher, Mrs. Bordoloi, seemed irritated as ever! It was 2:30 in the afternoon... and the whole class was on the playground practicing the weekly drill. It was a Saturday, a very normal day, till the hypnotic heady scent of the moist earth started throwing its enigma around and the western skies went wild with a thousand thunders roaring as if there was no tomorrow!

And then began the huge downpour with all forty of us rushing under an old banyan seeking an immediate refuge... Forty...

too huge a crowd to humble the great banyan's legendary hospitability!

Maya and I stopped for a while and decided to excuse the banyan. We ran and quickly slipped into a worn old shack close by. And by the time we could feel the roof above, we were terribly drenched.... We had barely managed to settle in and I noticed Maya softly wiping off her wet face with her soaked white handkerchief... I could sense that she was shivering... I looked up and for the first ever time my indolent eyes fell on her trembling cherry lips and I looked on.... With the drooling droplets off her jet-black curls my sight started rolling down her tender cheeks, her delicate neckline and then her moist bosom... I deeply sighed in a state of gripping intoxication and realised that she was no less pretty than the prettiest of the women I had ever known. And all of a sudden, I felt a desperate need to hold her close to myself and press my lips on to hers and quietly confess that I love her....

"Honey...! Enough! I am really getting mad now! Can't you think about anything else? Since yesterday you had just been talking about her. I still don't understand what's so special about this woman! Remember, while we were in college, you had once shown me some photographs of hers. ...Well, I vaguely remember her face, but I am still quite sure that she looked pretty average...."

Well, I wouldn't differ with Apu.... It has been more than fifteen years but nonetheless I still feel gripped in an unusual obsession with Maya. For years together, even I was under the impression that it was my sheer admiration for her that she was still fresh in my deserting memories. But in the recent days as I set myself out to explore my real self, for the first ever time I could appreciate that it is nothing but a deep sense of failure that still doesn't let the wounds heal....

The Secondary School Examinations were just round the corner. Maya and I hadn't met for weeks together. I was missing her like crazy. I believed that she was at home busy preparing for the exams. I was dying to catch a quick glimpse of Maya... I took out my bicycle and rushed to see her. She wasn't there. Her mother's security guard informed that she had gone to the nearby market to buy stationery. I followed but couldn't locate her there either. It was getting dark and I was returning home peddling my bicycle half-heartedly. On my way, a little ahead of the Municipal Library, in one of those quiet darkish lanes, what I saw remained for ages the most excruciating moment of my life! I just couldn't believe it when my dim eyesight fell on a vehicle parked along the lane to see Maya with her mother's young good-looking driver, Pradeep, in a rather intolerably intimate posture!

Weeks passed and the exams were finally over. It was vacation time... Doom Dooma had once again bloomed into its usual splendour of spring! Our folks were busy planning their holidays and joining hobby classes. But for me, life wasn't the same anymore....

It was getting awfully difficult to get myself out of the fatal depression. I didn't know who to go to! I wasn't sure if I really wanted to face Maya. For reasons unknown, I wanted her to feel guilty and confess! But Maya seemed totally ignorant. Probably on that fateful evening she couldn't clearly figure me out in the dark and gave herself the benefit of doubt. Eventually, even I decided not to pursue it with Maya at all and just prayed that I hadn't ever witnessed the hell! God, it was so hurting!

The pain continued with days of agonising severance and nights without a blink of sleep... I realised that I couldn't bear the distance.... Every moment of solitude, every hour of hollowness repeatedly reminded me that it was time for me to *forgive* her for everything and patch up... I had no expectations. I just wanted us to be together!

"Congratulations Siddhartha! You are really superb! Except for Mathematics, you have got the highest scores in all other subjects! In fact, if you would have scored a little more in Mathematics you could have easily been the topper! Never mind, I am sure you'll do it in your Senior Secondary Exams!" God, it felt so good to hear her voice! I wished I had never distanced myself from her....

"I hate to say this but I think I must tell you that probably today is my last day in Doom Dooma.... In fact, it is my last day here! Believe me; it just happened out of the blue. Honestly, I didn't have any idea about it.... It just came as an abrupt reaction from my Mom after seeing my results.... I agree that I had always been dreaming about it but I hardly could ever guess that I would actually be the State Topper! I am really too amazed Siddhartha, and so is my Mom! In fact it's she who wants me to go to Delhi and stay with Kalpana aunty, an old friend of hers who currently runs a women's hostel there. Siddhartha, I should have let you know about this earlier but you know... I am actually leaving tomorrow. Trust me; it will be difficult staying away from you... I will miss you Siddhartha, I'll really miss you.... And I want a promise... you will have to keep writing to me! Right Siddhartha...?"

The next morning I woke up at quarter past four. I realised it was drizzling outside. I peeped out through the window. It was dreadfully dark and misty. There was an unusual calm in the feeble rhythm of the drizzle.... It was getting on my nerves. The world around looked brutal... I felt thrown out by the fleeting time... I was nervous. I was strained. I wanted to flee. I wanted to howl. I wanted to scream... I wanted to confess to Maya that in spite of everything, all what I need, want and desire was being her man for the rest of my life!

It was half past six and the blushing morning sun had finally managed to wink behind the hulking haze. I looked up to watch the silver linings around the clouds. They seemed nearly missing... I took a deep breath, inhaled some courage and dashed to Maya's house.... Her mother's security guards and helpers were busy loading their vehicle with Maya's stuff. They were all about to leave for the railway station.... I somehow sensed that it wasn't the right time to split the beans... and hoping that the seven-page letter in my right back pocket would at least handle the basics, I meekly pushed it into Maya's lovely fingers and whispered a rather pensive goodbye....

"Siddhartha...!" Maya tried stopping me from the behind... For a second or two, her voice sounded irresistibly mesmeric! ...But my reluctant feet kept advancing.... She persisted, "Siddhartha... Why aren't you saying anything? What's wrong with you, Siddhartha? Have I offended you for any reason? Why aren't you talking to me? Tell me Siddhartha..." and I succumbed. But if you ask me today, more than the mesmerising effect of Maya's alluring voice, it was the overpowering vulnerability within my own self that I had fallen to!

I turned back and tried looking into Maya's puzzled eyes. She appeared all stunned and cold! I was baffled how she could read the whole letter in almost no time...! I kept staring at her expecting her to break the silence. But Maya looked further composed. She vaguely smiled and said, "I think I know what you have written in the letter. I will read it on my way to Delhi."

Maya's weird leer remained an annoying mystery till she finally wrote back.... Actually, it took her over a month to respond and my flimsy psyche over those thirty eight days of a rather fretful expectation went through a fairly severe state of palpable depression... But then, at last, the utter delight of seeing her mail in my letterbox made it all up for me!

I was holding the envelope with both my hands, staring it endlessly with all my affection, and was plainly relishing the bliss... And then, there was a gush of an eccentric fear and misgiving and I sensed a sudden fall. My thinned joys had left me numb and nervous. I wasn't too sure what I had landed up at....

28th July
Kamala Nagar, New Delhi
Dearest Siddhartha,

Apologies... I am sure you will pardon me for the delay.... And trust me; I am really sorry about that! But to tell you the fact, I didn't want to respond in haste! I wanted 'it' to get its due time and consideration. It definitely wasn't just replying a letter out of courtesy. Probably you might not agree but for me it was more than a mere dichotomy! I agree that a phone call was a definite possibility but I just thought that I would possibly express myself better over a letter….

I really wonder where to begin….

Siddhartha, you are just sixteen and so am I. Do you really think that this is the right age for us to decide who do we spend the rest of our lives with? Honestly, I think the answer is 'no'. We definitely deserve to make a matured, well-informed and wise decision on that, right? I am not saying that a relationship is not possible between us. Neither am I saying that you are not the right person... Siddhartha, it is just a matter of time. I think we should give ourselves enough time to grow up and let the relationship grow into its natural fold! Tomorrow, if both of us feel that our relationship demands a marriage, so be it! Let's not try hastening things… I'm sure you will appreciate.

Miss you loads!!!

Maya

July 29

Doom Dooma

Maya,

I am yet to understand whatsoever you have been attempting to express in your letter. Honestly, it is too complex for me to appreciate. If you ask me, all that I know for sure is that my only purpose in life today is to be your man. I just can't see life beyond... Maya please let me just once share my dreams with you…. You'll definitely know what I am talking about….

Maya, I don't know what you mean by 'giving ourselves enough time'! I think we have already spent sufficient time to know and appreciate each other. Why do you think we need more time? Are you by any chance trying to say that I might not turn out to be a good enough match for you by any means in the days to come? Maya, your one 'yes' can change my world! And believe me, success, wealth and power would just be incidental!

Do think about it and as you say, don't reply in haste!

I am sure, I don't have to say, how much I miss you.

Siddhartha

8th August
Kamala Nagar, New Delhi
Dearest Siddhartha,

I have always admired you for what you are! Genuinely, I do not doubt your capabilities at all! And let me make it very clear that 'success, wealth and power' is not what would dictate my decision of choosing my life partner. But there are a few other things that I can't ignore and I want you to be aware of it. You know that my mother through out her life has undergone hardships of the worst order to get me the best possible things in life. She had to absolutely sacrifice her own youth to win a life of dignity for me. Naturally, even she must have had dreams for me. And to tell you the truth, more than anything else, my mother's dreams are the ones that I genuinely cherish. Come what may, my only goal in life would be to make all of them come true!

There's something more that I want you to be aware of! ...Siddhartha, I definitely feel kind of reluctant to share this with you... but hiding it from you would be all the more painful....

Since I was in the Eighth Standard, I have been unusually attracted to someone... Probably, you already know the person... and if you do, I am sure you would find it a little difficult to believe....

I was fourteen and he was twenty-six when I met him for the first ever time at my mother's office. I being the only child of an influential political leader and he being one of the seven children of a poor postal peon, there was hardly much that we both could have in common. But at the very first meeting, I found him to be an extremely bright and ambitious person.... Something that I really appreciate in men... and furthermore, I learnt that he is an absolutely self-made man! Siddhartha you won't believe; even today he does all sorts of petty jobs to support himself and his studies....

I just hope his hard slog pays off soon! ...And why not? After all, the next year he is completing his L.L.B. to become a qualified lawyer! Although at the moment, he is kind of helping my mother in her community work, he strongly believes that soon he will find his own niche in the political circles as well!

Pradeep... That's his name! ...Trust me Siddhartha; he is a hero, a true hero!

Sometimes, I feel as if everything was pre-destined. He is such an alluring personality that I never even had to think twice... I just went getting further involved. To tell you the truth, it was rather impossible for me to resist myself from getting close to him! I was helplessly in love with him and lucky me, even he found me smart, matured and charming enough for a fourteen-year-old girl....

But as you know it, life is not a fairy tale.... My mother does not quite approve this relationship. She is certainly not too comfortable with Pradeep's background and neither is she confident enough that he would actually be able to make it big in life. So she just wants me to stay away from him for the time being and that's the reason she has sent me to Delhi. I love my mother and respect every wish of hers. I know it for sure that she is the ultimate architect of my life. I will blindly let her plan every move of my life. After all, she has always been a true champion!

Siddhartha, my mother has always given me adequate liberty in life. She has hardly ever tried to impose anything upon me. Unlike the parents of many, she has never tried turning me into a puppet of her whims and fancies. ...Tell me what's wrong if she expects me to be successful? And I am sure it is equally fair on her part to expect that I marry an eligible man! In fact, she has rather been pretty considerate! She has explicitly told me that if a few years down the line Pradeep manages to emerge successful, she wouldn't mind let me go with him! Actually, I believe my mom would be happy about it because though born to a Christian father, I have always been brought up like an orthodox Brahmin and it has always been her latent desire that I settle down with a

Brahmin name. Thankfully, Pradeep is at least a Brahmin! So, that leaves me with very little choice… I hope you would empathise….

Love,
Maya

The message was fairly loud… I spent hours reading the letter again and again; without really catching even a strain of possibility of becoming Maya's man. I realised that in the first place, I didn't match the criterion of being a Brahmin. Secondly, having been a sixteen-year-old at that point in time, being able to earn a conventionally esteemed status for myself too sounded like a matter of ages! However, with my very own opinion about Pradeep, and him as the benchmark, things still seemed pretty much within the realm of possibilities and I decided to stick on. And thus my focus in life started shifting from myself to the world outside. I too started aspiring for what million others do. I too began accepting mediocrity as my fate.

4

Dwindling Dreams

"HONEY…! Riz has been calling since morning... Why aren't you picking up the phone? Mind it honey; Major *Saab* won't spare you for this! *Loh*, just pick up the phone and talk to him…."

The phone ring was not loud enough to wake me up from my dream—a dream that had been haunting me for the past fifteen years… Invariably, it comes in the wee hours, towards the end of my sleep, and leaves me in absolute emptiness and confusion… I see that I am sleeping with Maya beside me and a sudden rush of passion turns me into a child and she vanishes into nowhere….

"You *bastard*, you better understand that you are being a real *ass*! *Saale, ek phone nahin uthaya jaata tere se? Bastard*…! I am so damn sick of your *fucking* histrionics! Tell me, will this ever end, Siddie? …You told me that you are on a self-exploration. I really doubt… I think you are exploring everything else but yourself! Come on now; stop being a jailbird of this disgusting nostalgia in the name of self-quest!"

Riz sounded fairly convincing… no less than what he used to be sixteen long years ago! Ironically, the debate over Maya still continues and Riz invariably manages to repress it, every time.

Indeed, things haven't moved much from the autumn of 1992….

I still quite clearly recollect; I was frantically searching for a copy of W. Somerset Maugham's *Of Human Bondage* at the local Municipal Library. Suddenly, at the issuance clerk's desk, I noticed a familiar face busy getting it's only copy issued in his name. I walked up to him to ask how serious was he about the book and he exclaimed back calling me by a name that a very few of my friends knew me by! I was stunned; it was Riz, the devil from my early school days in Darjeeling! We shook hands and he winked at me saying that I could take the book, as he was there just to check if Municipal Libraries happened to stock pornographic stuff! Idiot…! Pornography…? And that too in a government library! Shameless rascal…!

Riz's family had just returned to Doom Dooma after spending long years in the Himalayan town of Darjeeling. His father, who was a teacher in one of the boarding schools there, had opted for a voluntary retirement to start a school in Doom Dooma; his native town.

The Khans; Riz's parents were our neighbours in Darjeeling where both he and I were born almost during the same time of the year. We grew up together in the same locality, went to the same kindergarten and studied together in the same school till we passed our Fourth Standard. But in spite of this fairly long association, somehow, the possibility of a friendship had never really occurred to us. Probably, I was the one to be blamed….

As a child I never felt too comfortable with Riz's *weird* behaviour. If fun to him meant pulling down a girl's skirt during play, I preferred being at home listening to yet another fairytale from my mother. Indeed, we were too different….

Anyway, though accidental, our rendezvous at the library effectively ended up being a fairly pleasant one! More so for my selfish self as I presumed that precisely by the virtue of the old acquaintance I finally managed to catch hold of the book that I was crazily hunting for! I thanked Riz and both of us cycled back home together.

Riz's ancestral home in Doom Dooma wasn't too far from

the Municipal Library and came on the way to my home. I stopped by at his place, met his parents and spent some delightful time watching piles of old pictures from our Darjeeling days.

A week later, Riz came home to pick up his book. Over a casual chat he mentioned that he wasn't quite enjoying his new school... I was not surprised. For someone like him, Doom Dooma could actually turn out be horrendously unexciting! I sensed that he had already made up his mind.... He wanted to go back to Darjeeling!

"Doom Dooma is *fucking* sick! It has been more than a month here and I haven't seen a single good babe! Even the women out here are too uninviting... Leave all that... bloody... you don't even get good cigarettes here!"

We had several rounds of discussions on this subject and I kept trying with all my might to convince him to stay back but he was not the one to listen.

I was almost on the verge of giving up when one fine Sunday morning Riz came rushing as if he had something really exciting to share. He insisted that I come along to a place, which he said might be the only thing that could hold him back from leaving Doom Dooma! I was pretty stunned but didn't want to put across my surprise too openly. With a rather blank head I just took out my cycle and started peddling it behind his to ultimately land up at a place reasonably out of the municipal limits of the town. The place looked ordinary and just couldn't excite me at the first go.... It was a railway-bridge over a thin rivulet that separated Doom Dooma from the adjoining Defence settlements. I kept staring vaguely till Riz finally spoke up...

"Isn't this fun?" He winked and I kept looking on... I bluntly supposed that he was talking about the bridge and probably, at the most, the glitzy sun behind... I nodded and he stormed back, "What the *fuck* are you looking at? Idiot, look there, behind the pillar...." He pointed his finger at the broad wide mossy pillar right at the middle supporting the creaky old bridge and as my sight followed I saw a small group of dusky, stout middle-aged women, in bare minimum clothing, fishing in the knee-deep water. I felt rather embarrassed and lowered my sight in an uncanny reluctance.

"Don't tell me *bastard* that you didn't get an erection! …This is what I hate about you hypocrites! Why can't you guys just accept something that is so very basic and natural?"

Ignoring his candid remarks I quietly kept pondering on what he could have possibly seen in those ugly rustic females that he decided to stay back in Doom Dooma….

"Idiot that was a joke…! Well, now listen carefully… It's really something serious… After days of serious assessment, I have kind of decided that I shouldn't mind spending the next two years in this goddamn place. Now don't be under any illusion; it has got nothing to do with your persuasion skills! It's something more profound…."

I absolutely had no clue on what Riz was going to talk about. I just kept staring, indicating a sort of approval to go on….

"Do you remember Shyamlee M'am…?" And even before I could nod in affirmation, Riz continued, "*Yaar,* how could you forget Shyamlee M'am? *Arrey*, Shyamlee Sehgal; our English teacher in Darjeeling… She's here! I met her yesterday near the cantonment bazaar! Her husband is a Colonel now, posted somewhere in Manipur. She is staying here with her kids in the Army SF Quarters near the cantonment area on the other side of the river. Fucking good chance for me…!"

I was plainly shocked! And, *chance*? What chance was he talking about? How could he even think that a lady like Shyamlee Sehgal, in her late thirties, being a mother of two and the wife of a senior army officer would even approve of such a relationship? …And that too with a sixteen year old kid?

"Of course, that's the whole fun! You think I won't be able to screw her harder than her *fucking* husband? You don't know me, *idiot*! I have already done my homework right…."

"You remember Manoj Thakur, right? *Yaar wohi, apna Mannu…?* His brother, Rakesh, is now with the Assam Rifles…

Few months back in Darjeeling, when he was home for vacation, I learnt from him that Shyamlee M'am's husband, Col. Sehgal was posted in Doom Dooma for some counter-insurgency operation.... And if you trust the local rumours, all that while, that *fucker* kept getting into some creepy mess or the other... so much so that the Assam Rifles Headquarters had to intervene and get that *fucker* transferred to Manipur. And since last year he has been *fucking* around there!"

"Well... I was of the opinion that Shyamlee M'am had also shifted to Manipur along with her husband but yesterday while talking to her I got a different hint altogether.... Seems, she is not in very good terms with that joker! Well, that's of course good news for me but...."

"Hey, do you mind coming along...? I am going see Shyamlee M'am! She stays close by. She gave me her address yesterday. ...I believe their quarters are right across ... Siddie, you're coming, right?"

Well, in spite of being awfully opinionated against Riz's weird ideas, I began finding myself gradually engrossed in the tremendous conviction that each of his riotous strokes complacently generated... I realised, it was indeed hard to turn down his proposals, how much ever inappropriate they might initially sound like. So when I was asked to accompany him to Ms. Sehgal's house, I just ended up quietly following him.

"Hey Riz...! Come on in! That's your friend? Oh... he looks so familiar! Well, *lemme* guess... Siddhartha Kumar, right? Hey, so nice of you guys to have dropped in...! Come, come on in! And Siddhartha... long time *ya*...? ...So how have you been? Where were you all these years? I think you were in your Fourth Standard when your family left Darjeeling, isn't it?"

Ms. Sehgal went on as I stood hushed incalculably amazed at her stunning memory! I also did realise that Riz was absolutely not at fault; for this time, I actually found her to be an astoundingly lovely woman! Unfortunately, we never met again. But for Riz, that was just the beginning....

"Siddie, I am a little worried about Shyamlee M'am's altering behaviour…. You might not agree with me on this but in all her recent mannerisms I see an apparent craving for attention… I think that bastard is not taking enough care of hers! …Siddie, I genuinely wish I could do something… You know Siddie; ever since I have fallen for her I have always prayed that she dumps that joker and beds down with me. And today when the time has probably hit the ground, it's leaving me with a rather weird feel! I am afraid if my presumption about M'am being attracted to me is just a *fucking* illusion and if it is really so, let me tell you pal, I will be royally *fucked* by my own *fucking* stupidity! No *yaar,* I can't let this happen… I must talk to her…."

I always perceived that Riz's feelings for Ms. Sehgal were those of sheer lust and yearn! And probably I had gauged it right… but eventually his repeated claims of being a true lover actually started gripping me in wild bewilderment! I was honestly surprised to know that Riz was genuinely planning to confess his love to Ms. Sehgal.

"Buddy, finally the mystery is solved ! I won't say it's positive but it's not absolutely negative either! I would say there's still hope!"

I just couldn't believe that! It was sheer impossible for Ms. Sehgal to even fling out the vaguest signs of accepting Riz's proposal! But he seemed determined. With his unusual ability to promptly make sense out of the nonsense, he concluded that he had sufficient indications to his favour and he would exploit them to the best of his advantage to make things happen!

"Do you have any guess Siddie about what on this earth made Shyamlee M'am marry that *fucking* clown?—Well, the very fact that he is an Army Officer! She boldly confesses that ever since the day they got married, theirs has been a distressed relationship. Still, she says, she has been clinging on to the marriage because she loves the life of an Army Officer's wife! Silly…? Well, not really! It's a matter of personal preference and I wouldn't blame her for that! And besides, why should I? I think she's being reasonably honest… And do you know what she did when I finally opened my heart to her? She didn't utter a word. She quickly gave me a warm hug and whispered into my ears that she's my biggest well-wisher. She said she'll pray for me and await the day when I attain the standing of proposing my love to a woman twice my age! Now you *asshole*, don't you think that's quite an indication?"

"Well, as of now at least three things are pretty clear! A; that she has a troubled marriage and so there stands an opportunity for me. B; she genuinely likes me and C; that she loves the life of an Army Officer's wife! So I guess, the mandate for me is also equally clear! I am joining the National Defence Academy! …They say it's tough to crack. I am sure it is but only for those *assholes* who don't have Shyamlees in their lives to fire their drive! …Well I am all set and my preparation starts right today!"

Riz's resolve didn't surprise me at all. I had known him for years and in spite of my prejudices against him, I had always valued him for his valor. Even in those early days of our youth, he was for sure a man of action and not one of those who would gamble away his time weaving daydreams of feat and glory, drifting apart from tangible efforts. He was a fighter to his core and literally jumped at anything that even vaguely smelt like a challenge!

Though in my heart of hearts I constantly acknowledged Riz's unmatched determination, I found myself ridiculing him often deeming his hard work to be wasteful and futile. I kept doing so almost habitually till I finally realised that my actions were the sheer manifestation of a subliminal envy! I recognized that with every step of Riz getting him closer to his supposed goal, I was being constantly reminded of my utter failure to even set my target right! I was disturbed being unable to justify that if the mere guess that he getting into the NDA shall win him Ms. Sehgal can be so motivating for Riz, why couldn't I, in spite of my repeated self-vows, be a little more conscientious about proving my eligibility to Maya! I felt direly miserable and cried for solace….

"*Fucker*, who's this Maya now…? I am sure she must be a real *fucking* creepy female, for nothing exciting can ever excite you bastard...."

I was kind of nervous, but I couldn't help telling Riz how deeply I felt for Maya, in spite of her persistent indifference towards me and her ongoing affair with Pradeep....

"Now what the *fuck* do you expect when you know it for sure that she loves someone else? And what the hell do you expect from me? Okay hang on; are you by any chance trying to draw similarities between your *fucking* love story and mine! Sorry buddy, mine is a different story! I am working so hard towards it because I know what Shyamlee wants! In your case, even your *fucking* Maya doesn't know what she is up to? On one hand she says she loves her *fucking* driver and on the other hand she wants you to prove your worth! And what *fucking* worth is she talking about? ...The worth of being able to manage four *fucking* wheels with a *bloody* steering? Forget it Siddie, not worth the effort!"

Riz looked pensive. He started digging out his pockets haphazardly—a precise sign of his nervousness, and pulled out a curled cigarette from the inner pouch of the olive green jacket that he often wore.... Then holding it between the thumb and the fore-finger of his right hand, he continued, "Siddie, I honestly don't know how serious you are about this female! But what I can gather from your sob story, hmmm... sorry, I mean your love story, is that more than her it's her mother whom you are actually fascinated to! But probably you were too scared to convince yourself about this subversive idea and so you kind of agreed to settle with a compromise – I mean the idea of screwing the daughter instead, huh? Okay jokes apart... what is seems to me is a classic case of emotional aberration and you need to seriously evaluate it all over again! I am very sure; it is the persona and aura of her mother that initially attracted you to Maya and ultimately, I believe, the way she cunningly rejected your proposal further fuelled your affronted ego and then your desperate desire to possess her!"

Soon there was smoke all around. Riz had finally lit the cigarette with his vintage *Zippo* lighter. Although he kept quiet for a while, he constantly kept shaking his head, suggesting it sufficiently that he was not in a mood to listen. Probably he was too sure that he had reached the root! He took a deep breadth, tried clearing the smoke with vigorous hand movements and resumed, "Listen *fucker*, now if you trust my analysis, I suggest you do two things.... One, you give up on Maya and see if there's a possibility of exploring a relationship with her mother. If you see one, see how long the lust lasts! Otherwise, if you think, appeasing your wounded ego by proving yourself to Maya is the answer; then just go ahead... Ready, aim and fire! But a word of caution here; don't even expect that once you prove yourself to her, she'll be all yours. In fact, the same holds true in my case as well!"

"Anything's wrong, honey? You didn't talk to Riz for long! What did he say? You seem to be lost somewhere? ...Well I need to leave for work now. Call me if there's anything important, okay? ...Bye honey!"

Apu seemed to be in a rush. I tried stopping her from behind... no luck! But yes, she's right; I didn't talk to Riz for long... But how could I? The phone call had left me in such unfathomable thoughts that they kept leading me to further thoughts, all vague and futile. And somewhere around, I caught hold of a bit of mislaid reminiscence that finally stole me from the irksome ambiguity! It has been all because of Riz's sharp comments all along the undulating phases of my life that today at this point of time I see myself amidst reasonable possibilities of finding an answer to my years of chronic depression.

Now peeping down the past, it appears really hilarious that Shyamlee Sehgal, whom Riz never met after his Doom Dooma days, was actually the might behind pushing him up to the threshold of the National Defence Academy.

Soon after the results of our Twelfth Standard Board Exams were announced, Riz was a happy man. He had made it to the NDA and was all set to leave for Pune to join the Academy. But Ms. Sehgal was not to be seen. She had supposedly left Doom

Dooma. Riz did enquire at the SF Quarters but people refused to elaborate calling it some personal problem. Riz was unmoved. He looked cold and indifferent.... I guessed that the 'lust didn't last too long'... I was content over my friend's contentment though... Besides, I too was no less happy a man... After all, I was primed for the most treasured days of my life, eager than ever to join Maya in Delhi.

5

Illusive Aspirations, Futile Efforts

ON an awfully dry and burning morning, amidst dizzily encouraging thoughts, I landed at the New Delhi Railway Station with a few of my batch-mates from Doom Dooma.

We booked a filthy little room in a low-priced Pahargunj hotel, and the next morning, we went about visiting the colleges to collect admission forms. I was anxiously excited… After all, Maya had promised to see me near the North Campus. I was just too glad, never quite aware that it could turn out be one of the major turning points of my life….

Maya never turned up… I spent four days; frittering hours everyday at the Bungalow Road Crossing near Kamala Nagar, daring not to enter the premises of Maya's hostel, the gate of which clearly read "Men Not Allowed".

Eventually, the rather long wait took me beyond my panic and on the fifth day, I found myself at the small office-room of her hostel, introducing myself as a cousin of hers.

My entry into that rather protected area however seemed devoid of much struggle. The girls inside seemed friendly and justifiably excited over seeing a boy in their hostel…. Just about then, a maid in a magenta saree, bending forward and mopping the verandah pronounced in the air that Maya had actually left the hostel for good. A girl, who was reading a novel lying lazily on a cot in the verandah, waved at me and added in deep lethargy "*Pata nahin,* I have heard that she's going to Australia for her Bachelors…God knows…!"

The great betrayal…!!!

An accompanying batch-mate, who wasn't too sure about his compatibility with Delhi's extreme climate, was planning to try his luck in some colleges in Pune. I decided to join him. We went to the Railway Reservation Center, caught hold of an agent; paid him a two-hundred buck bribe to get ourselves two reserved sleeper berths in the Jhelum Express that was leaving for Pune the next day.

It was the 9th of June. Sounds like hot humid summer in any other part of India. But it was, in point of fact, a drizzle day in Pune. The temperatures were as low as 18 degrees. Cloudy, foggy, wet and cold, yet warm enough to receive thousands like us who were at the threshold of a new affiliation with the city that I didn't know would become my home for the rest of my life….

The reflection of the city's apparent hospitality flashed a sudden smirk on my face… and I decided to move on….

"Fergusson College" I whispered to myself.

A couple of days later, I was in the campus of Fergusson College, standing idiotically and slothfully pushing myself in the queue at the Admission Form Counter.

"God…!!! Such a long queue! It's intolerable… Mama had told me not to come. She was planning to send *bhaiyya* instead. I thought it would be fun… Now look at this."

"Look at me; I am all drenched! You at least came by car. My dad didn't even let me do that. He gave me just fifty bucks and told me to take the bus. I wasted almost half-an-hour trying to get one. On top of that it started raining. Thankfully, a school-friend saw me standing at the bus-stop and he dropped me here. Tell me, is this *gonna* be the story everyday?"

I turned back to see the two girls talking. The one, who caught my attention at the very first glance, was an arguably good-looking young lady; short, somewhat plump, fairish, square-jawed, thick-but-short-haired and evidently North Indian. There was a dash of uncompromising innocence in her smile and I kept turning my head at every possible pretext to catch quick glimpses of her inimitable beam and every time I did that I was getting alarmingly fascinated about the way she softly bit her lower lip with her pearly whites, leaving adequately noticeable dimples on both her cheeks.

Sharp at 10.45 a.m. the counter opened. Soon there was some actual movement in the queue. Within minutes, as I managed to collect my form and started reading it while leaving the counter, I realised that the simple-n-dimple girl had vanished somewhere. Even her face, slowly but surely, started fading out of my memory.... All what I could remember was the yellow sweater that she was wearing. I stretched my eyes far and wide but Alas! she was gone.

Hastily, I shifted my focus to the form that I was holding and started following the bright black-and-yellow signage that led me to an auditorium where completed forms were to be submitted. I looked around for the girl in the auditorium as well but no luck. I took a corner seat and started filling up my form.

One of the sections in the form asked for the subject that the applicant wants to specialise in and it left me in crazy elusiveness. Time was running out and I had to make a choice. There were repeated announcements that no submission would be accepted after one o'clock and I somehow recalled an old conversation that I had with Maya about the bright and smart students always opting for Economics and that was it!

Three days later, I was in Fergusson College again. It was an important day of my life. The final admission lists were out. Huge lists of names... put up on the boards displayed outdoor.... It was quite a task to search for a single name in those enormously large sheets of paper. I was lucky that it didn't take me much time to find mine....

Fergusson College had convincingly brought in a whole new world to me. From an unobtrusively tiny school in Doom Dooma to the country's one of largest and most esteemed academic institutions, the transition was quite a one. I was pretty much aware that I had to bring myself up to the expected standards and had started working hard on both academic and extra-curricular fronts to make that happen. But almost repeatedly, I felt a strange force pulling me back from going ahead... I was still being haunted by the wrenches of the past, so much so that at times I had to struggle fiercely to rescue myself from the clutches of Maya's reminiscence!

The hours spent in the college were relatively easier but the moments of solitude were fatal indeed. How much ever I tried escaping, my wounded ego kept me encaged in pointless frustrations.... By any means, I wanted to outperform Maya in every sense and gradually, I started believing that it was the only way to win her back....

My obsession with success was getting intense and I was evidently losing my prized tenderness. I wanted to sound ruthless and conceited and soon, even the romance in my poetry was evidently starting to make way for my arrogant outbursts...

The world stared at a timid glow,
Beheld it mellowing over the brow!
Emitting an aura that's so divine
The tiny blaze was all set to shine!
Wands of seasons failed to quench
The immortal spirits of the sturdy flames
Tests of time toughened its soul
Infused a passion that feels so whole!
The epoch of gloom's bound to vanish
When the sway of will's destined to flourish!
Adorned with glitters of sheer resolve,
The flare illuminates the skies above!
Spreading the wings of power & might
The vibrant flames go on a celestial flight!
A tide of radiance roars from the far,
Blazons in joy; the 'Birth of a Star'!!

"Hi...! You are Siddhartha, right?"

I just couldn't believe my fate! The smile-n-dimple girl was right in front of me, in the same yellow high-neck sweater!

"*Actually*, I read your poems on the wall-magazine. You write really well… I was just wondering who this guy could be! Your friend Sachin; he's from my school. He just now pointed at you saying that you are the one."

"*Actually*, I don't come to the college every day. You know, I stay a little away from the city. Are you new to Pune?"

The bell rang! I hurriedly lifted my sack and ran fast towards the Wrangler Building to attend the Applied Statistics lecture. I regretted that I couldn't even ask her name….

"*Arrey*, Poet-the-Great… what's up man? So, you are famous now!"

I tried acting ignorant but Sachin knew it all. Trying to overcome my small-town introversion, I gathered some guts and asked him if he could tell me her name.

"Mango Dolly!" He stared at me for a while and cracked his typical giggle. "Seriously buddy, that's what everybody calls her these days. *Kyun*, you didn't notice her mango-yellow sweaters *or what*? *Bloody*, she hardly comes to college and whenever she does, she comes in those funny yellow sweaters. What else do you expect us to call her? …*I swear!*"

"Okay, so you are a back-bencher *too*? Good. Now I have some company. *Actually*, I was wondering if you really know my name… My fault! I never told you… Well, could be yours too… You never asked me, hahaha!"

"*Actually* my name is Vishwaroopa, Vishwaroopa Singh. Sounds too *Rajput*, isn't it? Well, I am one but somehow I don't really like that name. It sounds like someone straight from the sets of some stupid mythological television soap…. My parents call me Dolly, and now most of the people around know and call me by that name only... I know, it doesn't sound great either but it's certainly easier to remember and pronounce."

"And guess what, now they have started calling me *Mango Dolly!* You know why? Because of that yellow sweater I was wearing the other day. You remember, *na*? ...All because of my granny... She *only* knitted it for me. She has an *impossible* fascination for the yellow colour! Poor Grandma...!"

Though sounds mean, Vishwaroopa, I mean, Dolly, came as a great consolation at that point of time, for she kept me just amazed for months together. At a time, when I was walking around to find ways of chucking off my sick nostalgia, Dolly's presence inadvertently worked like a profound healer.

Dolly was different; really different. She was not like any of the girls that I had been with in the past, including Maya. She was a woman of contrasts. She looked average but there was something strikingly infectious about her looks that intrigued many, including a few of those who called her Mango Dolly. Academically, she was mediocre but it was impossible to ignore her sharp intellect. She was not at all into arts, music or literature but she passionately inspired *admirers* like me to write, sing or paint. Though extremely talkative, chirpy and mischievous, she was exceptionally soft-spoken and well-mannered. True, she was just amazing!

My meetings with Dolly were reasonably infrequent. In fact, I was never quite deprived of the opportunities of missing her....

Often, my wait used to surpass weeks... And there used to be absolutely no means to reach her. She lived really far off the city and I never had the kind of guts to land up at her place... Of course, I could have tried speaking to her on her home phone but that option was never offered and I too was not really sure if it was appropriate on my part to ask for it.

Those were not the days of e-mails and mobile phones. So, the only way I could reach her was through letters... But again, I was not too keen about writing to her... probably, because at that point of time, I just wanted to relish the longing that I was gradually developing for her... It used to feel like love, almost like love. It was some sort of a feeling that was erasing all those emotions that so far had kept me sickeningly glued to Maya. It was indeed a different experience and I was just beginning to love it!

But once, this longing surpassed all limits. Dolly was away almost for a month. My idle hours were getting tired of waiting. I was getting restless and tempted to indulge myself in things that I was not too positive about… I had to struggle really hard to say no to some of my friends who did *drugs* and stuff... I was scared. I wanted to escape that mood… I started searching for ways to engage myself with something meaningful and positive…

On one of those days, while sitting beneath the famous *neem* tree in our college campus, I saw a smart dude with a pony-tail carrying a guitar in his hand, sauntering lazily towards the Amphitheatre. There were a few others who followed him. They too were carrying some musical instruments with them. It seemed they were a music band. I got somewhat fascinated. I started tagging them on. I saw them entering the Amphitheatre. I decided to wait outside and watch them. I realised that it was one of their usual jamming sessions. The guy with the pony-tail was the lead singer. He was good. I went on listening to the numbers they played. Original compositions... Unconventional... Catchy and reasonably melodious.

They played for around two hours and then started winding up for the day. I approached them. I greeted them with a casual applause. None of them seemed to be in a mood to respond. They were busy packing. I walked up to the lead-singer and introduced myself. He still behaved arrogant. I felt a little insulted and because I didn't want them to upset me further, I told them bluntly that their compositions sound good but they were rather pathetic with the lyrics. I told them that they badly needed someone who could help them with some better sounding words. And finally, I proposed that they had the choice of including me in their band.

Soon, I was a part of *Puneri Missal*. That's what the band was called.

Amusingly, it was Raagesh, the lead-singer and the most arrogant of the lot who actually made this happen. In fact, he too happened to share a similar opinion about the class of their lyrics, and so, though not thoroughly impressed with the samples I had shared, he was the one who kind of influenced everyone in the band to offer me the chance of penning down a few songs for them, of course on an absolute trial basis.

It was a band of four and I was the fifth one to join. Of those, Raagesh was the lead-singer, Joshua the drummer, Mandar played the synthesiser and Vipul was the lead-guitarist. Lyrics had always been a job shared between Vipul and Mandar and both of them were pretty convinced that the words just don't matter!

All the four original members of *Puneri Missal*, as individuals, were extremely gifted artistes. But as a band of musicians, in spite of their genuine and repeated efforts, they just could not overcome the amateurishness that apparently exemplified their work. Raagesh blamed it on the substandard poetry in their lyrics and thus, all of them were quite hopeful that my inclusion in the band might turn out some magic.

I liked the energy and the optimism in the group. All of them were ambitious and had wild appetite for success, which I could sense every time they talked about Vipul's maternal uncles, Alpesh and Jayesh Shah, who owned a recording studio named *Swaranjali* in Mumbai's Jogeshwari (East) suburbs. From the recurrent discussions, it seemed quite evident that all four of them were convinced to their core that if we manage to create some great pieces, within days *Swaranjali* would turn all of us into stars.

The mandate was clear; the band had to work towards a music album. We were all excited.... Mandar and Raagesh started their work around the fresh compositions and were busy experimenting on the tunes. Every one in the gang was exceptionally engaged. But the pressure on me was probably the most.... After all the future of the band was clinging on to my pen....

For two complete weeks, we met every day; tried new compositions, rejected many, reworked a few to ultimately shortlist six Hindi *jazz* numbers. We decided to call our album *Jhoomta Saawan*, meaning 'Jazzing Monsoons' in Hindi.

It was a bright sunny October morning when we all met near

Kamala Nehru Park to head for the recording of our title track at a local studio in Narayan Peth. It was such a great moment for all five of us, particularly me, as the track had come out brilliantly and all four of my partners were pretty appreciative about it.

Jhoomta saawan… Saawan mein jhoomti woh nadiyaan…
Nadiyon mein chhote-chhote naau chhode toone-maine
Beh gaye jaane woh kahaan…
Dhoop ke sunehre rang aankhon mein sajaake
Hawaaon ki khuli mahek saason mein basaake
Kabhi titliyaan pakadnaa baagichon mein jaake
Aur Maa se naa bataanaa khadoch-chot khaake
Woh suhaane raat-din, waise pyaare pal haseen
Aaj jaane kho gaye kahaan…

(The jazz of monsoons… and those streams in jazz…)
(The tiny little paper-boats that you and I had set to hover)
(To which unknown did they waft away…!)
(Eyes laden with flashes of the golden sun)
(And the breath imbued with the blooming fragrant breeze)
(Catching butterflies in the orchards, at times)
(Never letting Mom know of the bruises and scratches)
(Oh, those beautiful days, those moments of delight)
(In which unknown did they fade away…!)

Jhoomta Saawan became an instant hit among most of our friends in the college.

Inspired by the rather unexpected response, we immediately created copies of the recording and went to Vipul's uncles for seeking their help in getting us connected to the big banner production houses in Mumbai. Both Alpesh and Jayesh personally received the tapes from us and assured us of a quick feedback.

Weeks passed but there was no response. Finally, Vipul decided to visit Swaranjali again. Raagesh accompanied.

Alpesh was terribly enraged to see them there.

"What brings you guys here? Didn't I tell you that we will come back to you once we hear from the producers? Stop bothering us again and again. I and my brother have already done our bit. But just tell me, which producer in his right senses would ever entertain such crude and amateurish work? And Vipul, you will have to learn to be cautious of your opportunist friends, okay? You are just being too dumb! Mind it; these friends of yours are just milking your family's money and social contacts… There's still time, just shoo them away…."

The incident completely shattered Raagesh. He, in fact, stopped coming for the jamming sessions and finally declared his exit from the band. Mandar followed and roughly within two weeks our band went to wrack and ruin.

The First Term exams were almost around the corner and I was visibly in a very bad shape. I was just not prepared to face the exams. The hangover of failure and deceit was such that I could not concentrate on anything else; not even Dolly. In fact, I had just lost touch with her.

One fine Monday morning, as we were just a week away from the exams, I decided to go to the college library and spend the day there putting together some study material for my preparations. As I stepped into the hall, I saw Dolly sitting right across the huge study table. It felt really good to see her. I waved at her and she came running. We went to the canteen, grabbed a quick bite of the *famous* Bun-Wada-Sambar and spent almost an hour updating each other. She kept cribbing about her long bus travels everyday and asked for my opinion about getting transferred to a college closer to her house.

"*Actually*, I had no intentions of coming to this place. We are from Dehradun. And if you ask me, I would love to live there for my life-time. It's just that my Dad has been posted here for the past few years and he decided to move the family here. He thinks Pune can offer me and my brother better opportunities in education and career... As if I care about it…!"

It felt like a relief to meet Dolly after such a long break, though our conversation kept hinting again and again that it could be one of our last meetings. Although even the thought of her decision to shift to another college was making me feel terribly uncomfortable, I decided to hear her on without expressing my discomfort....

"You know what? I came to Fergusson just for my friend's sake. And look at her; she still hasn't come! *Actually*, it's not her fault. Her admissions and stuff are already done... It's just that her father's being stuck there for some final paper work. *Actually*, they are coming back to India for good. They have purchased a house in Pune and uncle's gonna work with some company here."

I was least interested in whosoever she was talking about but at that point of time, to have her around I could pay any damn price; so I let her go on....

"*Actually*, she's my best friend. And the most interesting part is that we both share the same birthday.... Yes, we were born on the same day, in the same ward of the same hospital! Actually, both our fathers used to work in the same plant in Abu Dhabi. It was a very small industrial township and on top of that we were next door neighbours.... Till our eighth grade, we went to the same school and sat next to each other in the class. ... God...! I just hope that she comes here soon and joins me. Otherwise this frustrating bus ride everyday is just killing me!!!"

A day before the exams, I was heedlessly loitering at the Admin Building, effortlessly trying to figure out if the seating plans had been put up on the notice boards. The campus was quiet as there were very few people in the college at that time of the day. And almost unexpectedly, I hear someone calling out my name from far behind....

"Siddhaaaaaaaaaaaaartha...!" Of course, that was Dolly. But today she was not alone.

Dolly was almost running to me while the girl with her was quietly following behind. Dolly looked extremely excited. It was visible that she was just not in sway of herself. I was sure that the girl with her was her friend from Abu Dhabi.

"Sid, guess who this could be? Of course, this is the friend I had been talking about all these days. Finally, she's here. She reached just yesterday. So tell me, how do you find her? Don't you think we look the same?"

I stared at both as if they indeed did but felt extremely uncomfortable expressing my genuine observation. Dolly's friend was undoubtedly far better looking. So I just kept quiet, smiling at both, allowing Dolly to go on....

"Even our names sound so similar; I am Vishwaroopa and she's Aparoopa! Believe me, as I always say, we are almost like twins."

"Hello Siddhartha...! Such a pleasure meeting you... Catch up later... I have got some work at the Admin Building. Besides, the exams are also starting from tomorrow. I need to get the notes photocopied and rush back home."

Aparoopa Chaudhury, contrary to Dolly's 'almost unquestionable' description, turned out to be quite another individual. I found her strikingly quiet, sober and focused. And after the exams, as I started spending more time with her, my admiration for her grew in leaps and bounds. Her unmatched charisma and her interestingly insightful approach to life, career and everything that mattered to us at that stage of our life kept me in complete awe of her.

Another thing that I found exceedingly mesmerising about Aparoopa was the way she carried herself. Even at such a young age, there was an incredible dignity in the way she dressed, behaved and conversed. She was an absolutely no-nonsense person and indeed too perfect for her age.

Soon, I started waiting for Dolly more eagerly than ever because now meeting her also meant an opportunity to meet Aparoopa.

Dolly didn't seem much uncomfortable with the new development though she hardly ever openly commented on it. And I too decided to be silent about it.

A month before the First Year University Exams, Dolly's family moved back to Dehradun owing to her grandfather's sudden demise. In fact, Dolly's father was supposedly in the midst of a property dispute with his brother and he had to rush immediately to claim his share.

All throughout the month of March and the half of April, Dolly stayed with Aparoopa's family. After the exams ended, on the 18th of April, after celebrating her and Aparoopa's birthday, she left to join her family in Dehradun. From then, almost for three years, we remained in touch; just through letters.

After our graduation, Aparoopa and I went to the University for our MBA programme. Dolly, by then, had quit her studies and had started teaching in a school at Mussoorie. Life had indeed set us apart in two different directions. The MBA programme kept me and Aparoopa obnoxiously occupied. Dolly, however, kept writing a letter or two every now and then but neither Aparoopa nor I ever had the time to respond.

We were approaching the placement season and the time was rather getting tough…

Those were yet not the days when employers would flock to the B-school campuses to woo their prospective recruits. All of us in the campus were in the worst ever grip of anxiety and all this while the strongest thought that dominated my mind was—where is Maya and what is she doing; rather, is she also struggling or she has already made it big somewhere! I was disturbed but somehow in my heart of hearts, I was also hopeful that the placement season might turn out to be a game-changer and thus I kept myself amused by the thought that just one good job-offer could be the end of my struggle to win over Maya. But the million dollar question was—Where is Maya and what is she doing? I tried all my sources but couldn't learn a thing about her. Of course, I was informed of rumours that she had an affair with a Canadian professor in the university from where she was doing her Mass Communications programme and that sometime back she had eloped with him to the US.

The placement season ended with a great deal of dissatisfaction among most of our course mates. But both Aparoopa and I somehow managed to get placed with reasonably decent employers. I got placed as a Sales Trainee in a Swedish manufacturing company and Aparoopa joined a local software firm as an HR Executive. We were happy to have been among the very few to be placed in Pune and we kept no stone unturned to make the best out of it. Though awfully busy in our respective jobs, we made it a point to catch up regularly over the weekends and left no shopping-mall, restaurant, discotheque or cinema unexplored over those days of our new-found financial independence. And finally, when we got tired of everything, we decided to get married.

6

A Second Chance

"WHAT are you saying Siddie? …Okay fine, but what's so *eureka* about it? I just refuse to believe that you never were aware of this! So many times I have heard you saying that you feel miserable about your failure to prove your worth to Maya, and today you sound as if it's news to you! I really hate you for this…. You just get too melodramatic about petty things!"

Riz was fuming and I decided not to take the conversation forward. Almost unwillingly, I hanged up. But this time, Riz had predicted it wrong. I was on a different track altogether… In fact, I was just about to tell him that after days of retrospection and self-exploration, I am finally here with the *truth*! And my truth is about the bundled dilemma of seeking my long lost dreams against the recurrent demands of reality. I wanted to tell him that if truth on one hand demanded that I stay focused and sustain our struggle to overcome our incapability to bless ourselves with our little ones and support a great future for them, on the other hand, truth also insisted that I do justice to my own self and seek to regain my lost passion and pride.

Truth also demanded that I acknowledge the fact that more than my passion, what I had lost to Maya in my past was my pride and I must win it back by proving a strikingly evident superiority in the present. After all, life doesn't always give everyone a second chance!

I realised that I was rather convinced to my core that whether pride, passion or both, the destination was irrevocably one—Doom Dooma, the place where jiffies of my past buried under the grime of time and latent reminiscence are still wide awake to wake me up in the zeal that I had been craving for since years....

Ever since my childhood, I had been seeing people in the family, the neighbourhood and others in the familiar pockets of the world giving up their present for the sake of creating a hypothetically secured future for their upcoming generations, who in turn also never fail to do the same for their progenies. At all times, this phenomenon seemed unreasonably frustrating... and all such encounters with potential compromises used to fuel a violent spark in me to run and escape the vicious cycle of middle-class forfeit! But today, when I am finally confronting the opportunity of making a choice, I am finding it to be a real tough one. Nevertheless, between family and self, without much thought, I am being pushed to choose my self—an irrationally bold move which would never have been possible on my part had my family been dependent on me by any means. Thankfully, my wife has a well-paid job and our entire liabilities together seem to be fairly insignificant being weighed against the resources at my disposal. Practically, there are no worries. But of course, I am being more than aware that this decision of mine could cut me off from the completeness of a conventional family life that almost everyone always desires of. However, an outlandish grin of optimism at the bottom of my heart was subtly attempting to convince me that things would be alright!

"Are you nuts...?" Apu won't spare me today... "This is shameless! How can you just come and tell your wife that you are going...? And where the hell are you going—Doom Dooma? But why Doom Dooma...? You just want to figure out what you want to do, right? Do it here. Take your break, go to Mahabaleshwar, stay at Chandrana uncle's cottage, freeze your plans and come back. Why do you have to go all the way to that *goddamn* place? I don't support this!"

"Ever since the first day of our marriage, I have seen this strange yearning in you.... Why did you leave that rotten place in the first place? You should have been happily squandering your *bloody* life there with that *bitch*... Just get lost Siddhartha. I don't want to see your face. Go to your *fucking* Doom Dooma and just *fuck* around...."

Having known Aparoopa for such long, I could sense the veiled approval in her unforgiving reaction and I quietly moved into my room, opened my steel cupboard to take out the good old American haversack that my mom had gifted me when I had left home for Delhi fifteen years back. It still looked amazingly neat... I unzipped the sack and started cleaning its interiors. I could feel Aparoopa standing behind but she chose to be quiet as I continued with the cleaning. Suddenly, I feel a hard thud on my right forehead and I fall abruptly with my back on the ground. Ouch!!! How could she do that to me??? Apu just hit me with the brass vase that stands at the corner of the entrance of our bedroom. God, it hurts!!! It's not bleeding though... but I can feel the blunted bulge....

"Go to hell, you *bastard*...." That's her emblematic way of saying "goodbye and all the best"!

My forehead was hurt badly but still I could not look for enough reasons to retaliate. In fact, there was no anguish. I was firm on Doom Dooma and certainly didn't like the way Apu reacted to it but I did not want to hurt her by any means. Probably, I still loved her as much as I always did. I wanted to tell her that it was just about searching my own self further and the passion and pride attached to it. I wanted to hold her by her arms and tell her that I love her. I struggled against the floor and strengthened my grip on the bed to climb up and slowly make myself stand on my feet.

Holding my head with both my hands, I started walking droopily towards the living room. Apu was lying still on the sofa. She saw me approaching but resolutely reserved her reactions. I kept advancing and finally grabbed her by her waist to hold her up to me. She was in tears. I felt distressed. Without a thought I pulled her close to my breast and took her into my arms. Soon we found ourselves on the bed, living those moments of intense intimacy that had treacherously crept out of our life years ago….

Soon, Aparoopa was deep asleep while I was pretending to be so…. Every passing second posed itself as a constant reminder of my resolve. It was quarter past two in the night and I finally managed to slip off my bed. I picked up three *khadi kurtas,* a couple of polo-shirts, my bathroom slippers and three pairs of jeans from the wardrobe and placed them noiselessly in my haversack along with my basic toiletries and undergarments. And finally, I lengthily searched my wallet to check if it had all what I needed.

I went for a quick shower and almost immediately changed into a pair of beige *fishing shorts* and a bright-red T-shirt. Quite unusually, I didn't put my regular deodorant-spray today as it could possibly wake Apu up!

I opened the door with sufficient caution, pushed myself out with the baggage and shut it almost without a sound. As I exited the elevator, I called up Shiv to know if he could drop me at the airport. I was planning to take the six o'clock flight to Delhi, spend a day with Riz and then catch the next morning's flight to Dibrugarh. I was kind of thrilled fantasising the wobbly ninety minute bus-ride from Dibrugarh to Doom Dooma, as Shiv sleepily agreed to oblige.

It was 5.15 a.m. and Shiv and I were at the airport. I walked up to the airline counter to check out for a spot booking but learnt that all flights to Delhi had been cancelled owing to bad weather conditions. I was upset. It seemed like a bad omen… I was nervous and I wanted to smoke. Alas, we were not carrying cigarettes!

We took the car out from the parking lot and started driving fast towards Pune Railway Station. I was on the driver's seat, pressing the accelerator rather hard, apparently venting out my disgust. Shiv was getting annoyed and he couldn't help shouting abuses at me. In a state of sheer excitement, I ended up bumping on to a car parked right in the middle of the road. *Shit*! This was the last thing I could anticipate!

"Hey, wait! Who's that *dumb ass*? *Lemme* just come out and *screw your happiness*!"

The voice sounded unmistakably familiar.

Gosh, that's Dr. Ujjwal Sapatnekar—the *Dream Reader*....

"Is that you, Siddhartha? Hey, I am extremely sorry about those wrong words. I was actually helping Sudha with her driving lessons. You know most of the times my assignments keep me out somewhere and she gets stuck at home. We bought this car for her last month but she's still not good at changing gears.... Never mind, but what are you guys doing here at this hour?"

I silently glanced at the dent on the bumper and turned my eyeballs hesitantly at Dr. Sapatnekar indicating a modest appeal to let me offer some sort of compensation against my imprudent act. Dr. Sapatnekar's smile got naughtier and he burst into a squealing laughter. "Come on Siddhartha! My practice still fetches me enough! And besides, what are the insurance companies here for?"

I was meeting Dr. Sapatnekar after a gap of almost six months. But his incomparable warmth left me convinced that he had always been around.

Dr. Sapatnekar is not a friend. In fact, it would be immodest on my part to call him so. For many of us in the corporate world, he has been an exceptional behavioural trainer, to a few he is an expert theorist and to a very select few he is, what we fondly call him—the *dream reader.* Having worked with extremely reputed universities, institutions and corporations across the world, Dr. Sapatnekar has now set up the Center for Better Living at Dehu Road, near Pune.

Dr. Sapatnekar as a consultant to our company has been an acquaintance since the past six years. But it was only in the last couple of years that we developed a strong personal bonding as well.

Dr. Sapatnekar hails from Bhopal. Music and arts come naturally to him. He is a trained Indian classical vocalist and a genuine enthusiast of Hindi literature. Though he has spent half his life across the most advanced parts of the world, he is amazingly rustic in his mannerisms and more than often he comes across as gullible and blunt.

Ever since we have been interacting, I have found Dr. Sapatnekar to be extremely passionate about dream analysis. He is a die-hard fan and follower of Carl Gustav Jung and he believes that working with dreams can actually change lives!

"*Bhai* Siddhartha, I know it wouldn't be so simple, but why don't you just give it a try. Start with recording your dreams on a plain sheet of paper. Keep doing it for at least four weeks. See if you can identify a pattern. If it looks too complex, bring it to me."

"Do you know that dreams are believed to be messengers of god? In fact, they, in a variety of coded forms, constitute a mechanism that constantly reminds you of thoughts and actions that need your immediate attention. God wants every human being to attain completeness in life. Hence, the broken pieces that you have left behind and the unseen ones lying ahead need to be searched for and brought together. Dreams guide your way to achieve this union...."

"But you need to be extremely cautious while working with dreams. They are just like the juvenile children. If you ignore or abandon them, they will turn violent. It is therefore extremely important that you embrace your dreams, listen to them carefully and try to understand what they are trying to convey. You will be amazed that this will lead you to answers of questions that you had always been haunted by! *What say? Ho jaye*?"

I never had doubts on Dr. Sapatnekar's expertise but the concept of 'working with dreams' always seemed convincingly mysterious and scary. Honestly, I was not too keen and Dr. Sapatnekar never really forced me to do so.

"What happened, Siddhartha? Why do you still look so anxious? *Arrey bhai*, I told you, I am not going to charge you anything for this dent? Come on, cheer up! But on a serious note, is everything okay, Siddhartha?"

I asked Dr. Sapatnekar if I could join him for tea at his place and winked at Shiv, suggesting him to push off with the car.

"Okay… so that's the matter…! Siddhartha, do you mind spending some more time with me. I am relatively free today and I was thinking of doing a clean-up at my centre. Why don't you just join me? I have a cosy little outhouse inside the centre's premises and we can talk there more freely about your problem over a mug of beer! And buddy I promise you; I won't talk about dreams. Does that help?"

Soon, we were on the Pune-Mumbai expressway; racing Dr. Sapatnekar's good old black SUV. And as we passed the Wakad By-pass, I noticed the huge collection of music albums, mostly those of Beethoven, Mozart and Pandit Ravishankar lying on the rear-seat. I pulled out one of them and tried inserting it in the player. Dr. Sapatnekar stared at me for a second and smiled….

"You like music?"

I nodded.

"What else do you like?"

I couldn't help telling him how much I hated being asked about what I like and what I want to do in life. I bluntly told him that he is probably the millionth person on earth to have asked this question and I was genuinely not in a mood to respond.

"Siddhartha, please don't get me wrong! I am asking you this question because I am confident that I have the answers to all your problems, provided you cooperate…. Okay, if I say you have the freedom and choice, what are the three things you would like to possess, do or chase? Well, if that still sounds irritating, let me put it in other words; if I have the might and the will to give you any gift that you ask for, what is it that you would be asking for?"

My answer was straight: Peace of mind, a sense of fulfilment and a high self-esteem.

"And what do you think would get you these? More to the point, what makes you feel that going to Doom Dooma or for that matter any other place in the world, would help you achieve these?"

"Look Siddhartha, many a times, we don't understand what the real thing is! Many a times, we chase a thing, possess it and then realise that we never wanted it. At times we hate a thing and just give it up but over the years we realise that we actually quite liked it and we start endeavouring to relive it. Look at masturbation for instance. In your early teens it was fun. Gradually you realised that it was some sort of a consolation. A repeated sense of consolation turned it into a frustration and then you wanted to have the real thing. You found the real thing. Experienced it, enjoyed it, and redid it over and again to realise that you still need to masturbate. In fact now you like it better than the real thing! So tell me darling, what is indeed the real thing?"

Dr. Sapatnekar's analogy had left me in complete awe! I was wondering if all my theories on self-exploration and cerebral masturbation were absolutely baseless and unjustified!

"Siddhartha, I strongly feel that so far whatever you have been doing under the name of self-exploration is highly motivated by your wounded ego. Tell me honestly, you just want to teach her a lesson, right?"

Without further thoughts, I could plainly agree that Dr. Sapatnekar was entirely right.

"Okay, forget it! Are you in touch with her? Do you have any idea about what is she doing now? Do you think she is still waiting there for you to come and convince her that you are worth a billion dollars or that you are equally or probably more successful than she is? ...It's no use sitting here assuming! Go and find out where she is and what is she doing?"

I tried my best to persuade Dr. Sapatnekar to understand how important it was for me to stand above Maya's current standing. I agreed that I was committing a mistake by mixing pride with passion but I was also equally convinced that it was my lost pride that ultimately compelled me to abandon my passion.

Suddenly, there was an abrupt right turn and we were at the entrance of Dr. Sapatnekar's centre. It was an impressively maintained facility spread over an acre of lush green farmland right on the lap of the foothills of the magnificent Sahyadris.

As we alighted, Dr. Sapatnekar looked a little composed. He skilfully maintained his symbolic smile but it was evident that he was in the midst of some computations. He hurriedly turned towards the outhouse and started searching for the keys in his pockets. As we entered the place, he ordered his assistant to get some wafers and nuts along with two beer-mugs.

There was a small fridge placed along the Burma-teak sofa which lied majestically in the front room of the cottage.

The only other room in the cottage had a bed, a table, a chair and a cupboard in it. There was a small kitchenette and a toilet attached to the bedroom.

I was leaning on the sofa and Dr. Sapatnekar was instructing his assistant on the menu for lunch. As he was doing so, he also continued his struggle to connect his laptop to the internet cable. The assistant left and Dr. Sapatnekar brought out two cans of some unknown brand of German beer from the fridge. He opened the packets of nuts and started popping them into his mouth almost immediately. He handed me a can and continued....

"Where were we, Siddhartha...? Yes, passion and pride. Okay, so what is your action plan for Doom Dooma? How do you think this trip will help you regain your lost passion and pride?"

Honestly, I didn't have an answer. All what I knew was, by going there I could at least be better informed about Maya's whereabouts. And as Dr. Sapatnekar also concurred, I wanted to track her and find out how far had she gone in life. I wanted to evaluate if it was still possible to vie with her and prove my true worth.

"Well, that's the *pride* part of it; what about your passion?"

Well, by then I had realised that my current passion was all around regaining my pride by any means and it didn't really matter anymore whether or not I succeed in identifying and pursuing my genuine interests. And all that I could understand at that point of time was the fact that no matter what I do and how successful I become it would not be of any use until and unless it bore a direct relevance to Maya. As regards to success; I had achieved ample of it in my career, but how did it matter to her! The question was not about success. Rather, it was the question of being able to do what Maya was doing and of course doing it better than what she is capable of!

"That still doesn't answer my question, Siddhartha! Okay, just imagine that you have already managed to make Maya realise that you are the biggest thing that she has ever missed in her life and she agrees to make up for the blunder she has committed, what is it that you would still like to pursue as your passion for the rest of your life?"

I didn't know again but Dr. Sapatnekar's ruthless interrogation was compelling me to think for an answer. Music–I said. But I was not too sure. Or may be I can write lyrical poems that can go into music albums... Anything interesting... creative and exciting....

"Look Siddhartha, it is absolutely not a problem if you don't know at the moment what you really want. In fact the solution lies deep within the fact that you are trying to explore your goal in life, which not even one percent of the world's total population ever does. My only worry is that you do not set off on a wrong track. Please stay focused. And keep exploring with all your might. I am hopeful that soon you would find yourself there."

I could sense what Dr. Sapatnekar was trying to hint at but I was rather too obsessed with Doom Dooma to think otherwise.

"Well, I should not try to influence your thoughts any further. Frankly speaking, I believe it from the core of my heart that the secret of self-quest can not be taught over a crash course. It's a journey that every self-conscious individual must undertake on his own... I genuinely pray that your trip to Doom Dooma drives you ahead in your quest."

Without paying any serious attention to what Dr. Sapatnekar was feverishly trying to communicate, I stood up in haste and asked him if I could use his internet to send an urgent message to my wife. He shook his head in abrupt agreement and pushed his laptop on the table softly towards me. He understood that I had already frozen my plans....

I started typing, as Dr. Sapatnekar looked on, a very brief e-mail to Aparoopa informing her about my decision to spend the next couple of weeks in Doom Dooma. I apologized for being a little secretive about my plans and promised her that if things worked out, I would be back soon.

While writing the e-mail, I observed that the words came pretty spontaneously and there was not a bit of regret or shame about what I, knowingly or unknowingly, was getting into!

We finished lunch in almost no time and I was all set to go. I picked up my stuff and requested Dr. Sapatnekar to drop me at the Lonavala S.T. Bus Stand from where I planned to take the bus to Dadar.

By then, I had changed my travel plans and instead of the Pune-Delhi-Dibrugarh route, I settled on to catch the direct flight from Mumbai to Guwahati the next morning at eleven.

I left Lonavala at quarter to four and reached Mumbai by around six in the evening.

I had to pass the whole night in Mumbai and wasn't too sure if I could turn to any of my friends there as I didn't really want too many people to know about my plans.

I took a cab to Santa Cruz and booked myself at a hotel reasonably close to the airport.

The next morning, after having breakfast at the hotel, I called up my boss Kalra on his mobile phone. He picked up immediately; in fact at the very first ring. I was cautious that I should start without letting him say a word but he turned out to be smarter....

"Hey Siddhaaaaartha...! What's wrong with you my boy? Why and where did you disappear? We all are just too worried... Had there been any problem, you could have at least shared it with us! Tell me, what are we here for? I don't know what you really think about me but to me you are much more than just a team-member, Siddhartha! Do you really understand that? Is it that you have taken up another job? Have you been offered a job abroad? What is it Siddhartha, tell me my buddy?"

I didn't want to cook up any story to waste his and my time and told him rather candidly that I wanted a sabbatical.

"Sabbatical…? Well, that's fine but for how long…?"

I was not in a position to be even distantly specific and keeping him in any sort of false hope also seemed incorrect. So I told him that it could initially be around six months but it might go beyond that as well. Kalra was silent for a while. Having known him for years, I knew that he didn't want to express his displeasure but he was certainly not too comfortable with the idea of letting me go on sabbatical!

"Okay, but who knows, you might as well feel like coming back within a month's time! May be it's just that you need a long break… Well, whatever it is, I just hope that you come and join back soon! Just send me an official e-mail on this today and I would take it up with the HR folks. Hopefully, we should arrive at some solution. Don't worry!"

Kalra's unofficial approval came in as yet another booster to my expedition. I felt energized as it seemed that things were kind of falling into place.

Indeed, it started feeling like a great beginning….

7

Chasing Maya

THE craft landed at Guwahati airport at around two o'clock.

It was raining outside and my eyes hungrily stretched out of the misty window to catch a glimpse of the world that had been out of my sight for the past so many years.... Interestingly, I had to remind myself that I was no stranger to this place.... It was my hometown, Guwahati!

An abrupt flash of old memories of summer vacations spent with my grandparents, hours of leisure squandered with my cousins and the slothful feel of long siestas over the idle humid afternoons, filled my heart with sweet nostalgia. And suddenly, the thought of my old and lonesome parents being completely unaware of my arrival left me with an awful strain... My heart longed to see them....

I was carrying just one hand baggage and it didn't take me much time to get out of the terminal. As I stepped out of the arrival lounge, my eyes were stunned with the grandeur of the startling greenery. It was springtime and Guwahati could not have looked better!

I walked up to the Pre-paid Taxi Stand and decided to go and meet my parents....

Over the forty-five minute drive from the airport, I befriended the driver, Manoj, and asked him if he could arrange for a vehicle for my travel to Doom Dooma. He took down my father's phone number and promised to send a car with his younger brother, Dilip, positively before eight in the evening.

It stopped raining as I started approaching home. Upon reaching there, I stood at the outside porch and rang the doorbell with some sort of disinclination.... My father slowly opened the door and peeped out in yawning indolence. Probably he was in the midst of his afternoon nap.... He kept gawking at me and looked just too shocked to see me alone. He shouted for my mother impatiently and kept questioning me if things were fine and if everything between me and Aparoopa was all right....

Actually, I could not blame him for that as in the last eight years of our marriage this was the first ever time that I had travelled home without her.

I attempted on my part to change the topic, but my father was getting all the more hysteric. He called me insensitive and idiotic, blamed me for the supposed failure of my marriage and asked me to go back to Pune immediately. After persistent efforts, I finally managed to convince him that I was on my way to Doom Dooma to attend a function. I told him that some of our school mates had organised a reunion there and after attending it I would fly back to Pune the very next day.

Mom still looked apprehensive but didn't say a thing... She straight away went into the kitchen and started cooking something on her ancient frying pan.... The aroma was pretty familiar... Yes, my guess was correct; it was the filling for the delicious chicken sandwiches that she used to make whenever in my schooldays I troubled her to make something interesting for me!

I stretched myself at the divan in the living room and kept ogling at everything in the house; particularly my parents and it seemed as if the world had not changed at all!

The sandwiches were ready and I quickly grabbed them and started hogging as Mom kept updating me on all the weddings, births and deaths that took place since the time we last met. Right then, Dad intercepted and asked me if I was doing anything about *going the family way...* Suddenly, there was a calm that stayed for a few seconds and I nodded hesitantly to avoid a precise answer.

I told Mom to quickly make some *Khichdi* and scrambled eggs and told her that I would need to leave for Doom Dooma by around nine in the night.

After a while Dilip, the driver, called up on my Dad's phone to check the address. Amazingly punctual by Guwahati's standards, he turned up with an old white shambled Tata Indica exactly at 8:30. I was impressed!

I hurriedly finished my dinner and much to my parents' disappointment, left home immediately. On our way, we stopped at a petrol pump towards the outskirts of the city and I gave Dilip a thousand rupee note to fill the diesel. And even before he could come back from the cash-counter, I dozed off....

By the time I woke up, we were just a few kilometres away from Doom Dooma.

It kind of felt like a dream... *The captivating sight of the crowning greenery, the glittering golden drops of the morning sun, the narrow serpentine lanes of tar vanishing into nowhere...* Every little thing from the times of yore was right in front of my eyes.

Soon, we were in the town. And my famished eyes started gazing around again to hog the sight of objects and faces that were a part of my life years ago. I remembered Maya and sighed in deep vagueness. As we drove ahead, I noticed that except for a few new shops and one huge concrete structure, which appeared like a shopping complex, everything else looked just the same.

I recollected that the place where that new concrete structure stood was once the home to Doom Dooma's only decent hotel Paradise Lodge. In fact all the while since I had started from Mumbai that was the place I was intending to stay at... I was lost and didn't know where to go now.

It was too early in the morning for Doom Dooma to wake up into action and I was desperately looking out for someone who could help me find an accommodation. I told Dilip to stop the car near a tea kiosk and asked him to find out if there were good hotels around. The man in the kiosk shook his head and pointed out to a road-side eatery on the other side of the street. I came out of the car, reframed Dilip's question and asked the man if he could suggest a place where I could stay for the night.

"Sir you can go to Hotel Maya; the one behind the ASTC Bus Stand. That's the best hotel here."

It took us hardly two minutes from there to reach Hotel Maya.... It turned out to be a decent four-storey building with an elegant entrance and beautiful ambience. I checked in and bade goodbye to Dilip, handing him two crisp thousand rupee notes.

I was given a room at the third floor of the hotel which faced the erstwhile Winston Road. That was the street where Maya used to live with her mother.

I stood at the glass-window and my eyes started searching for Maya's house. I located one with a red tin roof that shared great resemblance. I called up the room service and ordered breakfast. After a little while a young Nepali boy came in with three slices of toasted bread, a cube of butter, a boiled egg, one banana and a flask-full of tea. As he finished placing the plates on the table and hastily turned to exit, I stopped him from behind and asked him if he could tell me whose house was that....

"Sir, that's our owner's house. Mr. Pradeep Sharma, the owner of this hotel owns it. He is also the local MLA."

I finished my breakfast and went for a long shower. It felt refreshing... Quickly changing into a pair of jeans and a *khadi kurta*, I walked out of the hotel for a stroll. I crossed the street, walked up to a *pan* shop at the Winston Road crossing, picked up a packet of cigarettes and made an effort to chat with the folks lingering around the shop.... None of them really seemed interested but I kept pursuing. A middle aged man who was busy fixing his cigarette-lighter resting his right foot on the municipal garbage-bin appeared like an easy catch. I approached him and asked him in the local language if he could help me locate the residence of Indranee Goswami. Without even giving me a glance, he just started off with the directions to which I added if he could also tell me whether she was in town.

"In town...?" He sounded really irritated; and added in fury, "She is no more in this world! The house that you see there was where she used to live. Even this hotel; Hotel Maya belonged to her. She passed away last year in a road accident.... Now Pradeep Sharma owns all her property."

On being asked about Maya, he seemed almost ignorant.

"We haven't seen her for ages. I think she lives somewhere abroad."

Not getting enough clues about what had actually happened; I went to the house that once upon a time used to be Maya's home. It was locked. A security guard, standing at the gate, informed me that Pradeep Sharma was in Delhi for some official work.

I came back to the hotel, ordered lunch, finished eating and went for a nap. I woke up a little late in the afternoon and ventured looking for familiar names in the telephone directory. Alas! that too turned out to be an utterly wasted effort. Frustrated, I went out again for yet another stroll; this time towards the livelier part of the town.

I spent two long hours at Prabhat Restaurant waiting desperately to spot a known face in the crowd.... Having failed for yet another time, I decided to go to Crown, the only bar in Doom Dooma, for a nice chilled beer.

It was a dingy little gloomy place that played distasteful Hindi songs from the eighties and served the cheapest possible brands of liquor. I sat on a corner table and ordered my beer, looking around again for at least one known face. Suddenly, I saw a tall dark man entering the bar. For a moment, I was tickled; he looked like one of our classmates from school. He too glanced at me and passed on. I concluded that it was not he. But within seconds, he came back and started staring at me again. And as I lifted my face to look at him, he howled in joy....

"*Arrey yaar* Siddie *tu*...? So what the *fuck* on earth brings you back to Doom Dooma?"

That was Pareekshith Naidu; an insignificant creature from our batch who was never known to anybody by his real name.

His anglicized nickname 'Porrie' was so popular that nobody ever took the pains of knowing his actual name.

The skinny, tall, dark-complexioned Porrie, who all along his school days fantasized himself as a Punjabi-speaking Pathan from Delhi, was one of the biggest laughing stocks of our times. What made him all the more irritating and often left him in deep embarrassment was his unmatched love for writing 'Hindi romantic poetry' or what he at least supposed to be so. I still remember how passionately he used to share the *shayaris* that he had written to express his wild emotions for his Bangladeshi maid-servant, Nazia.

Nazia ki yaad mein tadapta hoon main
Hanstee hai woh, to tapta hoon main
Jab bhee meri jawaani ka josh mujhe satae
Mujhe Nazia, bas Nazia yaad aae

(I get restless at the very thought of Nazia)
(Her impish laughter leaves me in sheer lust)
(Whenever the fire of desire arouses me)
(I want Nazia, just Nazia by me)

Porrie's father Venkateswara Naidu owned a small transport business in Doom Dooma. They were a family of four—Porrie, his younger brother Sreejith and his parents; all being strikingly different from one another. The father was just too mechanical a person, the mother an active social worker, Sreejith a brilliant student and Porrie just good for nothing.

My rendezvous with Porrie at *Crown Bar* did not end up being as boring as I had initially anticipated it to be. Of course, all the credit goes to Porrie! It was he who brought up the topic of Maya and asked me if at all I was in contact with her. I didn't say a thing but understood from his gesture that he too might have been one of her old admirers.

"You happened to be very close to her.... We always thought that there was something going on between the two of you. In fact, I personally suspected that you guys were probably married to each other until I learnt from my brother that she's in the US."

I clarified that I was married to some other person and I had not been in touch with Maya at all ever since the day I left Doom Dooma.

"Now I of course know that, buddy… You remember my younger brother Sreejith, right? He is now in the US. He is doing his Ph.D. in Biotechnology. Last October, I was there with my mother to see him. And guess what, I met Maya there. She is also in the same university. If I remember it right, she is also doing her Ph.D. there."

I was excited. My heart was dying to hear more about her but I had to resist my impulse from getting too obvious.

"Siddie, I don't know but everyone in the class always felt that you were smarter and more intelligent. Maya was good…. But come on, you were no less bright! Buddy, I am no one to comment and I am probably too less educated a person to say this but you too should have gone for something similar, man! Please don't get me wrong, I am sure you are doing far better than most of us but America, Ph.D. … all that sounds so great, isn't it?"

Knowingly or unknowingly, Porrie had sparked off another fire in me. He was right, what was I doing in life? I started assessing… a Ph.D. from US could not only place me at par with Maya but it would also give me a tremendous sense of achievement. Nonetheless I realized that having being utterly bored of my job, pursuing a Ph.D. could definitely prove to be a welcome break!

"I am sure you would know plenty of people there but do let me know if you need any information about the universities out there. Sreejith before leaving for the US had done an elaborate homework on the universities and lot of his friends had also sought his help before going there. If you say, I can connect him to you…."

It didn't sound like a bad idea at all. It reminded me that over the last couple of years, two of my great pals Tanuj Sharma and

Dheeraj Kumar were behind my life persuading me to quit my job, take the GMAT and join them for a Ph.D. Tanuj was in Boston and Dheeraj in Baltimore. Both of them were my batch-mates from MBA. Tanuj was working in Delhi for a British multinational and Dheeraj was with a European bank. Both of them had given up their extremely lucrative jobs to get into their long cherished career in academic research.

Though Ph.D. was probably the last of all things that I could have imagined doing, I was enthused at the thought of the possibilities it carried along. And by the time I finished my beer, I was almost sure of my next steps! I took down Porrie's phone number and left for the hotel.

The next morning, I was all set to leave. I just wanted to meet Porrie once more to get the address and other details of Sreejith.

I had a valid multiple-entry US Visitor's Visa and going there on a recce trip did indeed sound like a great plan.

"Are you serious? I didn't know that I could be so influential with my words! Thanks for making me realise that, buddy! Any way, here's his address... Carbondale is a very small city. The population would be hardly around twenty-five thousand and you would find a lot of Indian students out there."

I was impressed with the way Porrie was passionately trying to help me out and I in turn lent all my attention to make him feel even better.

"There aren't too many Indian restaurants but the one where you would find all *desis* and Pakistanis flocking in the evenings is a famous joint called *Babaz.* You see, most of the restaurants in Carbondale are located in the South Illinois Avenue, just south of the train station... and *Babaz* happens to be one of them. There's a guy by the name of Baba Menon, who owns it. He's a good friend of Sreejith but trust me he's a real *asshole*. He's also pretty close to Maya. In fact that's where I had met her when I was there last year."

I couldn't tell Porrie what kind of a favour he had inadvertently done to me but I thanked him for all the help and walked out of his office with a spirit that I was completely alien to....

A week later on the 22nd of April, I was in Mumbai, all set to leave for the US.

It was the flight at 2:15 a.m. to London from where I had to catch the flight to Chicago. I was excited but all along the journey, a dreadful impatience kept troubling me and I groggily passed my time gulping down at least half a dozen cans of *Heineken*.

On the 23rd, I landed at the O'Hare International Airport, Chicago. My good old friend Rajdeep came to receive me at the airport. I told him that I was on some official trip and had to leave for Carbondale at the earliest.

"Well, in that case, I would suggest you take *The Saluki,* tomorrow at 9:15 in the morning; I mean... the Amtrak train to Carbondale. That will be really convenient... You know, Carbondale by road is actually not very far from Chicago. But I am not too sure if you would really like to drive down.... And don't worry; Amtrak is cool and it would take just around five hours to reach there."

I spent the night with Rajdeep's family, called up Sreejith to update him on my arrival and the next morning, I left for Carbondale by *The Saluki*.

Sreejith was at the Carbondale Amtrak station; standing with a placard that read 'Welcome Siddhartha *Bhaiyya*'. He was not the dark, lean, spectacled Sreejith of his childhood. He looked pretty well-groomed and trendy.

Much bewildered at his new persona even before I could raise my hand and wave at him, Sreejith came running and hugged me. He picked up my baggage and led the way to his bright red *Chevy* parked outside. Indeed, he turned out to be a darling!

Sreejith and I spent the whole afternoon chatting about Doom Dooma, our school, the teachers and everything good, bad or ugly about that place. He also updated me on his experiences around doing a Ph.D. from an American university.

Sreejith was an interesting person to talk to but all the while we were talking, my mind was constantly pushing me to ask him about Maya. Finally, I succumbed to my temptation and enquired in a rather composed manner if he was in touch with her.

"Oh yes, I meet Maya *didi* pretty often. We are in the same university. She is in a different school though."

Sreejith didn't speak further. Even I remained silent for a while. But having realized that he, unlike his brother Porrie, would not voluntarily blabber out everything, I decided to be a little more direct. I told him that I was on a recce trip and my target was to meet all of those friends and acquaintances who were doing their Ph.D. in the US. I stressed that while I was in Carbondale, it was very important for me to spend time with him and my good old friend Maya, as both, to my fortune, were Ph.D. scholars.

"*Bhaiyya*, this is your first day here, so I thought I will take you out for dinner.... Normally, I cook at home but on special occasions we do go out. And mostly, to *Babaz,* the hot favourite of all desis and Pakistanis here.... Trust me *bhaiyya*, you too will just love it!"

I smiled and nodded to Sreejith but the sheer lack of enthusiasm was evident in my eyes. Sreejith caught it immediately. He was a smart guy.

"Bhaiyya, I am taking you to that specific joint because invariably between six and nine in the evening, on any day of the week, no matter what, Maya *didi's* only address on earth is *Babaz!*"

It was 5:30 and we were already at the doorsteps of *Babaz*... A tall, dusky Indian gentleman in a black Jim Morrison T-shirt with fairly long-n-curly jet-black hair came out wearing a meek half-smile on his otherwise blissful face. He gently shook hands with Sreejith and gave a vague glance at me. I smiled and he spoke up in his polished manly voice....

"Deepesh Menon! They call me Baba... Come on in. There's enough space inside. All yours... take the corner you like...."

We started following Baba, as Sreejith began introducing me....

"Baba, this is Siddhartha Kumar from India. He was my senior in school. He is here for some work. Actually, he is a friend of Maya… I got him here because I thought it would be easiest to catch her here…."

Baba turned back and nodded with his half-smile.

"So Mr. Kumar, what would you like to have? Hmmm… please do not go by my last name. I do not serve anything South Indian. You can choose from *parathas*, *kheema*, *anda bhurjee* and *biryani*… that's it…!"

Except for the food and the owner, there was, in fact, nothing Indian about Baba Menon's restaurant! It was set up in a typical rustic mid-western ambience. It did however have a faintly Afghan and confusingly Persian tinge to it as well. Probably it was the *sheesha,* the Persian *hookah,* at the reception that was making all the difference.

I was still in the midst of my observation when Baba called Sreejith inside the chamber adjacent to the restroom of his restaurant.

Sitting alone in the restaurant, I continued observing the exceptional blend of beauty and ruggedness in some of the antique pieces at display. Suddenly, the bell attached to the entrance door rings. There was a visitor…. A short lady, almost concealed in her black overcoat…. She was wearing a black cap, the hood of which was nearly covering her face as she started speaking….

"I am sorry, I got a little drenched. This mid-western climate… so unpredictable! God, the rains are really bad this time. You know the Mississippi's already flooding!"

She didn't sound like an Indian. And before I could ask her to take her seat, she rushed fast towards the restroom. It seemed that she was pretty familiar with the place.

I went inside the room where Baba was sitting with Sreejith to inform them about the visitor. While I entered, I saw Baba rolling something in a piece of paper…. It looked like some narcotic stuff but I didn't express surprise or anguish over it and came out of the room telling them to come fast and attend to the lady.

"*Arrey* Maya *didi...!* Couldn't you recognise your friend? That was Siddhartha *bhaiyya*! ...And what *bhaiyya*...? You too...?? Come on, you guys are crazy! You know what; it didn't take me even a second at the Amtrak station to recognise Siddhartha *bhaiyya*. I thought you guys were such great pals... Forget it!!!"

"Siddhartha...? Siddhartha from Doom Dooma...? Oh yes, that's right... But your face has changed.... So how come you are here? No..., I mean..., I am, of course, glad to see you but...."

I sat down at the table where Maya was sitting. She ordered a *masala chai* and I looked on. I was trembling and my throat was drying up. I kept struggling hard to speak out all that I couldn't... In fact, every time I lifted my face to catch a glimpse of the face that once depicted my destiny; I saw a distinct indifference that discouraged me further from saying or asking a thing. Thankfully, she started off, though in the same frame of indifference....

"So what do you do, Siddhartha? And where do you live?"

I was just about to respond when she got a call on her mobile phone. It seemed it was personal. She walked out of the restaurant to take it. I waited inside and just kept waiting. She never came back. Meanwhile, the restaurant was getting crowded and I decided to call it a day. I went inside again looking for Sreejith and Baba, and this time I found them actually puffing *chillums* of *ganja* in that dim lit smoky little wooden chamber.

My guess turned right... Baba, under the cover of an Indian restaurant was running an illegal drug business! I stared at Baba with all the hatred and sarcasm. He didn't react. He just stood up and turned his blissful face at me. His characteristic half-smile still lingered on. Slowly, he put his hand around my shoulder and guided me to another corner of the room where two leaf-green bean-bags rested idly under an antique lamp-shade. Baba made me sit on one of those and settled himself on the other. He looked at Sreejith for a while. Sreejith left the room. Baba pulled one of the wooden stools in the room and placed it between both of us. He started digging out some weird looking stuff from the white canvas bag that hanged on his shoulders and placed them on the stool one by one.

"I don't owe you any sort of an explanation but I would definitely want you to know that this is not my business. I do not do it for money. I am just doing what I believe in. And I don't force my belief on any one. I entertain only those who come here with the same belief. No impositions, no conversions! It's all about helping my fellow believers seek bliss, seek their own-selves and seek divinity. If you think that's immoral, unfair or unjustified, that's your problem because I am just too ingrained in this profound belief of mine."

I was in no mood of an argument. Besides, I felt it was far below my dignity to discuss philosophies with a drug peddler. I was in some sort of a distress that was bothering me from within. For sometime, I thought it was the jet-lag. But then, I realised that I was rather too disturbed about the way Maya behaved and I felt a massive need to speak to her at the earliest. In spite of her apathetic attitude that visibly came out during those few minutes of our meeting, I rather regretted more about the fact that I couldn't even look at her face properly and talk to her for sometime... I walked out of *Babaz* in sheer disgust and started rambling around for a cigarette. I realised that finding a cigarette would not be easy in the US and sauntered back shamelessly to ask Baba Menon for one. While on my way back to *Babaz,* I inertly recalled the words of Baba Menon about seeking bliss and divinity. Almost abruptly, I felt a subtle need to try doing it. It was a wild thought but after rounds of further thoughts, it didn't sound like a bad idea at all. I concluded that it could possibly be the only way to stand the impending atrocities that the night in all probability had treacherously seized for me.

"Mr. Kumar, are you sure about it? I hope you understand that this is not legal in the US.... Well, you are absolutely safe at *Babaz* but please be aware that anything illegal in the US can put you behind the bars...."

I nodded imprecisely and hinted that I wanted it.

Baba started digging his canvas bag again. He pulled out a small white packet and a few strips of thin white paper.

"I don't keep the hard stuff. I don't even touch them. I hate chemicals. This is different, this is *marijuana;* nature's blissful gift to mankind! You might not agree but there is something incredibly divine about these amazing herbs...."

I shook my head suggesting my affirmation and observed Baba Menon meticulously rubbing and mixing the *grass* with pinches of tobacco that he took out from a sleek white tin container. His half-smile remained unaltered.

"By the way, I can see an eccentric misery looming on your face! Is that what you are trying to get over? If that is so, my friend, you will soon find yourself miles above it! That's my promise! After all that's what the divine bliss is all about.... It will grant you the freedom from all miseries of life.... Now, tell me something; can you see that handsome friend of mine from Lahore? He is Sakir. He is already in his divine bliss. Both you and Sakir are in the same room, but believe me, he is on a different plane altogether. And from the plane on which he currently is, everything looks, sounds and feels trivial, even his miseries!"

Finishing his *enlightening* sermon on divine bliss, Baba started putting the *grass*-tobacco mixture on a tiny strip of thin white paper, which he called *rizla*, placed a thick hand-made paper filter on one end of the strip, and began rolling it finely with both his hands to make the whole thing look almost like an even cigarette. He lighted it with his antique lighter and passed it on to me....

Holding it between my thumb and my fore finger, as I began puffing it like an ordinary cigarette, Baba caught my hand and exclaimed....

"This is not a cigarette! So don't smoke it like one!"

Slowly, Baba's voice melts down and he changes his tone to that of a spiritual healer....

"Smoking *marijuana* is more than just a pleasure; it is a divine act! It's your means to seek divine bliss! Try to bring in that element of divinity.... Come, I will tell you how you do it… Just hold the thing loosely and bring it gently to your lips…. Close your eyes and press your lips a little hard on the filter. Suck…! Suck it with all your might. Come on… go on…! Good! Wait!!! Hold it! Don't exhale. Hold it for sometime…. Let your thirsty soul embrace the divinity! Now release it, let it flow out gently… It should feel like a perfect ejaculation. Feel the calm, relish the bliss... Yes…."

Baba was right. It was not a cigarette. It was certainly something different… It was dull, it was not exciting… It was not fun… But it was peace… It was bliss!

I took another hard suck, held it long for my soul to embrace it and released it slowly to feel the perfect-ever ejaculation and I was at bliss, true bliss. Everything; everything on earth, right from my job, my onerous life, my escape from it, the chase for my passion and pride, Maya's indifference; everything just seemed too trivial… trivial to the extent that I ended up spelling out everything to Baba, a stranger whom till then I hated for everything that he was!

"Don't regret my friend for speaking your heart out! That was your sheer innocence! It is the divine influence that has awarded you with this exceptional innocence! You have vomited out the negativity that was killing you from within. Your soul is perfectly pure now. You are at bliss! You have attained divinity!"

Sometime later, I found myself lying on a bed, smiling at myself and the world around. I was feeling thirsty and struggled terribly hard to get off the bed and fetch some water. I went back to sleep and woke up the next day sometime around noon. I was at Baba's residence; a shabby little two room apartment….

I freshened up and changed and Baba came into the room with two huge mugs of freshly brewed roasted Columbian coffee. The half-smile still persisted but he looked a little concerned. He sat by the bed and bent himself towards me, as if wanting to ask me something. He looked on but didn't utter a word. He started sipping his coffee and slowly leaned against the bed. After minutes of deafening stillness, he finally broke the silence….

"Siddhartha, you might not be aware but last night, after the *joint*, you spoke up about a lot of things.... Some of those did sound adventurous and interesting but I am not too sure about your plans.... You said you have come here to evaluate the idea of doing a Ph.D.... Sounds good; but what I could gather from your rather unexpected eruption last night suggests otherwise... I don't think a genuine urge to do a Ph.D. has brought you here! It's something else.... And if that is so, mind it my friend, you are doing great injustice to yourself. It certainly would not be the end of your problems; rather it would create further problems for you...."

I was stunned... I struggled recollecting what all I had thrown up the night before... It felt extremely embarrassing but I somehow managed to look on without really lowering my sight....

"So, it's Maya, isn't it? Buddy, I wouldn't blame you for anything but please help me understand what did you mean when you said you want to prove your worth and win her over? Look Siddhartha, I would be very honest and upfront; you are just wasting your time. You are married, well-established and seem to be quite an okay person! Why do you want to get into all this? I sincerely suggest that you go back to India and start your life afresh!"

Baba Menon's new avatar as the mysterious well-wisher did not come as an easy gulp. I was rather astonished about the sudden compassion gripping the insensitive drug-peddler.

"Excuse me Siddhartha; but let me tell you that no matter what you achieve on this earth; whether you reach the stars or ravage your life proving yourself a thousand times and beyond, this is one woman who would never ever be won over! If you are still not convinced, just go ahead and try your luck...."

Baba's harsh words just failed to do the magic and I assumed it was only in the state of intoxication that he sounded concrete and convincing. On second thoughts, I felt like being challenged... It seemed as if he too like Maya had underestimated my worth!

All of a sudden, an unforgivable sense of offense coupled with a dire need to make things happen ran through my veins and I promised that I would not let myself down….

All this while, as I was cursing and vowing, Baba was quietly gauging my rage. He was silent. He was still. His blissful half-smile was intact.

His abnormal calm was getting on my nerves and I wanted to escape it. I tried running out of his sight and he caught me by my sleeve.

"Don't run with rage, my friend. You will get tired of it! Try running with your spirit; you will go places! I can say this for sure because I am one of those dumb idiots who ran with rage; so much so that everyone around started calling me *Panther*....

I was the *Panther* who had the reputation of never letting his chase flee.... Once by sheer ill-luck, I ended up missing one. It was just too insulting and I felt the pressure to live up to my reputation. I kept my chase on. Ultimately, I was there, with my chase right in front of me. I was thrilled at my accomplishment. I was looking all around to see if the world had witnessed this spectacular act of bravery. I was shocked. I realised that my rage had brought me so far from the world that there was no one to appreciate my triumph! More importantly, there was nothing anymore that I could really chase! I was humbled. I became a rock. I became Baba; Baba—the rock."

8

Dark Circles

BABA'S repeated words of caution seemed to make no impact on my obsessive self.... In fact, I was entirely in the grip of my *rage*; just too desperate.

The craving to meet Maya and gauge her current worth was so overwhelming that I was driven to plead Baba to make no more delay... .

Baba called up Maya to check if she was at home and within ten quick minutes he dropped me at her place.

Maya stayed alone in a nice big apartment in a locality that only the most affluent in Carbondale could afford. I stood in front of the door, inhaled deep and inspected the surroundings to confirm that I was not dreaming.... Then, trying to gain some poise, I walked closer to the door. I realised that I was trembling again. I was nervous. I was scared. But I was unmoved. I knew it deep inside that I was there with a purpose and nothing on earth could stop me from accomplishing it! I stepped a little closer and finally knocked the door.

The response was not too quick.... It took some time for the door to open.

My eyes were tirelessly stuck to door and finally when I heard the inside latch clacking, I felt an abrupt tremor within. I was almost dead... and I closed my eyes in a mysterious unease. And by the time I dared to open them, Maya was at the door, smiling at me. I smiled back in sheer restlessness and she called me in.

As I entered the apartment, which was certainly not as impressive as the exteriors, I glanced at her from the behind and observed that she had grown a little chubby... She looked fairer than before and her voice sounded much chirpier than what it used to be sixteen years ago. It was just too different a moment and I was absolutely lost.... And almost in that state of sub-consciousness, I hazily grabbed a corner of the room and placed myself feebly over a cushion that was lying on the carpet below.

Maya turned back and yelled, "Hey, why don't you just sit comfortably on the sofa?"

I lifted my head to a degree and somehow gathered the courage to make an eye contact with her. And if the partial glimpse of hers that I had stolen the night before could be ignored, this was the first ever time in the last sixteen years that I had seen her complete face. I stood speechless for a while for she looked a completely different person. She looked aged. Her face appeared wrinkled and there were dark circles around her eyes. But quite strangely, she still looked attractive! Probably, the clothes that she was wearing were adding a different flavour to her attractiveness....

"Siddhartha, I have got some left over pizzas from last night's party. Do you mind if we have them for lunch now? And of course there's some nice Mexican beer for you. Beer's fine, right?"

She was getting the stuff out of the fridge and putting them on to a plate for heating.

As she walked across the kitchen to place them in the microwave oven, my eyes indolently relished her smooth waxed legs and the curves that her white low-waist shorts were boldly revealing.

In a while, she got the pizzas out of the oven and walked towards the corner where I was sitting.... She started laying the plates on the floor and I was getting up to volunteer my help. I was almost up when my rather ill-behaved sight fell on her arrogantly inviting moist cleavage! In fractions of a second, I found myself speechlessly standing and rolling my greedy eyes all over her.... Suddenly, every part of hers and every gesture she made appeared to be laden with lustful allure! Even her bulky waistline, the dark circles around her eyes and her wrinkly face began driving me fanatically wild.... My heart started howling like an insane beast and I prayed hysterically to have her in my starved arms. I stared at her like a famished wolf, caught hold of her by her arm, dragged her face on to mine and began kissing her with all my yearn.... She didn't resist.... But she didn't seem involved either. I tried all the tricks I knew but nothing really worked. After a while, though I was just refusing to give up, she gently pushed me aside and threw herself on to the sofa. She started sobbing. I went close to her and tried hugging her again. She opposed. I pushed myself back on to the floor and sat down shamelessly without counting a moment of regret.

Hours passed and there was no movement on either side. Everything just stood standstill. While on one hand, I was adamant that I would not leave her place without winning her consent, she on the other hand was equally stubborn about not letting her good old lover-boy even advance an inch further.

It was getting dark and I stood up to switch on the lights in the room. Maya, pretending to be asleep all this while, got up moodily, cautioning herself from my *dreadfully unpredictable* moves. I got intolerably annoyed and asked her if she really hated being appreciated... I argued bluntly that I had not come to provoke her to sleep with me and tried convincing her with all my strength that I was in the US to evaluate the idea of pursuing a Ph.D. from an American university. I told her explicitly that my trip to the US was focused on meeting friends and acquaintances who were already into research programmes and upon learning from Sreejith that she also happened to live in the same town, I thought of seeing her for the sake of the old times. I overtly conveyed that though I still found her to be an extremely attractive woman; I was in no mood to resume any sort of a relationship with her!

Maya heard me out thoroughly wearing a distinctively anguished look that left me wondering about her next possible retort. I however looked on....

"Siddhartha, it seems you still haven't forgiven me...! *Jesus Christ*...! Even these sixteen long years could not heal your wounds! Please go back Siddhartha; please don't make me feel so guilty. I beg of you, please...! Whether you want to do a Ph.D. or you go to hell, I don't care.... But please get out of my sight. I feel really terrible!"

There was a sudden pause and Maya tried her bit to gain some control over herself. She quickly wiped the tears off her wrinkled cheeks and prepared herself shakily to resume....

"Look Siddhartha, you must still be in a frame of mind to explore and experiment but if you ask me, I am really sick of all that. I have had enough of them! Now words like experimentation to me mean nothing more than uncertainties and I have no more courage and patience to chase them anymore! And you can't blame me for that...! Tell me my friend, what else you would expect from a woman who has just been cheated repeatedly by destiny! I am telling you honestly Siddhartha, I don't know of any other woman on this earth, who has been married thrice, divorced twice, lived in with three men and two women and still been alone all her life...."

Maya's candid revelations came as a huge shock as I was absolutely unaware of those developments. I had always assumed that she was married to some Canadian professor with whom she had eloped from Australia....

"Now I know it for sure Siddhartha that it's your curse that has turned my life into hell.... But tell me honestly Siddhartha, had I ever told you that I loved you? I always considered you to be my best friend! I used to share everything with you... I never used to hide anything from you. For god's sake, tell me Siddhartha, what made you feel that I could accept you the way you expected me to? Even in the very beginning hadn't I told you that I was committed to somebody else? Hadn't I told you about Pradeep, the very first time you had proposed to me?"

I was taken aback. I didn't have answers to any of the points that she raised. In a way, I was convinced that she was right. I began realising that all this while I was living in a fool's paradise. I was living in a complex that was self-created.... I was unnecessarily complicating my own life! I felt ashamed and disgusted!

"But in a way, I think that you are right! My life would have been far more in shape had I accepted you right in the beginning. After all I always knew that your love for me was selfless and untainted. You have every right to hate and curse me. Indeed, I am the one to be blamed! But Siddhartha, now that life has given me a chance to apologise, I hope you will allow me to do so...."

"It's not that I was never too aware of what I had done to you when you had come to join me in Delhi. I am sure you must have not forgiven me for that bungle! But believe me; I was actually compelled to do so. Of course, when I had left Doom Dooma for Delhi, I had no intentions of getting into anything with you. I was just impatiently waiting for Pradeep to complete his L.L.B.... I was so deeply committed to start a new life with him... But destiny had something else in store for me.... The two years that I spent in Delhi turned out to be the most testing times of my life.... On one hand, I was tired of repeatedly disallowing you and on the other, I was feeling increasingly threatened by Pradeep's growing indifference towards me.... There were constant rumours about his alleged relationship with my mother and ultimately I went into an untamable depression with my mother's shameless confession confirming her illicit love-story!"

"By the time you informed me about your plans to join me in Delhi, I was already in shambles. I did spend some time considering the possibility of starting afresh with you but my conscience didn't allow me to let you bear the burden of my past... I wanted to escape... I wanted to go away from every-thing... Pradeep, my mother and you! But trust me; I had no wrong intentions for you because I always admired you, genuinely!"

Maya was sounding genuine.... And gradually, a feeling of profound sympathy started grabbing me compellingly....

Maya walked into her kitchen and made some tea. When she came back to serve, I could still see her beautiful waxed legs and her round warm curves; but somehow they didn't mean the same anymore....

"I lived in Melbourne for four years. I studied Mass Communication, got married to my fifty-two year old professor and came to Connecticut where he had picked up a teaching assignment. While in Connecticut, he decided to go to Canada. He was dying of leukemia and wanted to join his ex-wife and children in Winnipeg; the place where he actually hailed from. We got divorced and I got married to one of his Indian students; Advait Paranjpe. We moved to Houston, lived there almost happily for a little more than two years.... Advait's parents were never aware of our marriage and he never had the guts to tell them that he had been married to a divorcee! That was when life gifted me my second divorce! I left Houston, went to Jersey City, lived in with an old friend from Melbourne, Zubin Bharucha, and then with another friend, Yogi Patel. I got introduced to a colleague of Yogi, named Jenny, with whom I shared an apartment for a couple of months. Jenny came out to be a lesbian.... Her male-bashing stories and her irresistible charm got me immensely fascinated to her and we ended up in a relationship. While living with Jenny, I met Shannon; an ugly lesbian *bitch*... Shannon attempted wooing me on several occasions and finally one night when Jenny was out for dinner with her colleagues and I was alone at home, she stormed in, threw at me all her nasty seductive tricks and I just succumbed. We eloped. Interestingly, Shannon came in as an angel in my life. She was a great human being and was the only one who guided me with some direction in those days of my feral turmoil. Following her advice, I applied for a Ph.D. and came here to Carbondale to pursue it. Carbondale has been no good either. On my very first day in that town I met an awfully attractive man... your friend, Baba Menon! Looking at him. I felt as if my hunt for the perfect life partner had approached its end. But luck eluded once again and though we did live in for sometime, things ultimately didn't work out with him either. Eventually, in sheer disgust, I gave up all my womanly desires but that too didn't serve any purpose. My reputation turned out to be my biggest enemy.... It followed me wherever I went.... There are so many beautiful young girls out there! Why don't they just go to them? Am I that attractive? Or it's just that they find me an easy catch!"

"But now, I am not bothered anymore! Now, at least, I am married! And I don't plan to get divorced this time. You know, we do not stay together, but I know it for sure that I have a husband... and he is someone whom my mother had chosen for me. She found him through a matrimonial portal just a few weeks before she passed away. So I am very emotional about it.... He lives in Seattle. He is, so to say, *impotent*, but nonetheless; he is very important to me. I don't love him and I have never attempted to know if I mean anything to him but I have a genuine feeling that he is going to be my husband for the rest of my life! And of course, I do admire him for one reason. He has given me the kind of space that I want and that greatly matters!"

Listening to Maya's experiences turned out to be more than just a distressing encounter. It was an eye-opener. I recalled Baba Menon and realised that all this while I was just blindly *running with rage*. I was completely ignorant about what the *rage* was all about! Having known what Maya had gone through, my *rage* against her seemed absolutely baseless.... I cursed myself at my ignorance and turned to Maya to say good-bye. I looked at her and felt within me a strange sense of compassion. There was no rage, no chase and no lust. There was no urge to win over. I shook my face indicating my exit and she held her hand up shakily to stop me....

"Siddhartha, if I have the right to ask you; do you mind staying over here for the night? Actually, I realised that I felt deeply relieved talking to you today.... And I'll be happier if you could spare some more time with me.... In fact, in the last fifteen years or so, this is probably for the first time I have opened my heart to anyone and I'm glad that it's you. What I just now saw in your eyes is something that I had never seen in any man before.... My eyes are accustomed to lust, indifference and hatred and I have really hated men for that. In the morning, when I saw you being just exactly what I perceived all men to be, I couldn't control my fury. For a moment, I just forgot that I have also been equally nasty with you in the past and I had no right to expect you to be fair! But now, if I have rightly read what your eyes are conveying, I can safely assume that you have forgiven me. Haven't you?"

There was an unadulterated innocence in Maya's expression and I softly responded my affirmation. With sparkling drops of tears rolling down her dark circles, she held up both her arms hinting a hug and I quietly took her into my bosom. She wept, shrieked and laughed beyond control as I tried comforting her, caressing her tousled hair.

It was an appallingly touching moment and in a state of extreme effusion I decided to confess to her about the actual intent of my visit. I told her how my inability to prove my worth had stripped off my pride and passion and how it brutally enraged me to regain them. I told her about my self-propounded theories and how they drove me into my *run with rage*.... And as I emotively narrated my experiences, I saw in her eyes the same compassion that I had felt for her a while ago.

"Do you know Siddhartha; what has been the biggest problem with me?" And without expecting me to answer her question, Maya continued. "I never had a purpose in my life. Today, if you look at me, I am just nowhere. People would find it hard to believe that I had been a topper throughout my life! One would also not accept that I was a classical dancer or a singer. Today, I am just a jobless marijuana addict, who doesn't even have the count of people she has slept with! And you know why and how this has happened? Simple; I had never looked at life as a whole. I was just focussed on bits and parts. What I presumed to be goals were mere materialistic chases. But now with all my experiences, I have learnt that the secret of a good life lies in its completeness."

"Every human is a seeker by nature and in the absence of a meaningful goal turns into an untamed wanderer. It is exactly then one single-mindedly starts chasing material success and worldly possessions.... Proving your worth, outperforming others, self-obsession and greed are just some of the visible manifestations of this phenomenon. But this leads one to the vicious cycle of mediocrity and in due course results in depression and frustration. On the other hand, the one who listens to the soul seeks the real goal of one's life and attains completeness and true happiness. But mind it dear; because every soul is unique, there is no fixed formula for attaining completeness and true happiness!"

Maya simply stunned me with her truth-seeking deliberations .... There was some sort of a resonance.... And I realised that she was sounding almost like Sapatnekar.... The same theory about *completeness and true happiness*.... She sounded convincing but it was impossible to believe that someone who heedlessly carried the impression of a marijuana-hit nymphomaniac could sound so philosophical and yet so relevant and practical.

I was merely compelled to surrender my insignificant self to the vast ocean of knowledge that I saw unveiling and asked Maya to clarify what she exactly meant by *completeness* and if it was same as success.

"Often people confuse completeness with success. But, in the real sense, success, at best can just be an element of completeness.... And as I said, every soul is unique! Hence the core needs of the soul also vary from individual to individual. To a few, it can be *peace*. For some, it can be *knowledge*. It can also mean *power* and *prestige* to many. For most, it is a blend of all in varying proportions. But more importantly, it's about the spheres that human beings live in and interact with. Family, workplace, hobbies, relationships are a few common examples. Attaining completeness in life requires one to feel complete in each of the spheres that one is part of; and that ultimately brings the soul to the state of fulfilment and results in lasting happiness!"

Maya's analysis sounded perfect. But what I failed to understand was the fact that in spite of being completely knowledgeable about the possible solution to her chronic problems, what was it that kept her constrained from practicing her own theory in her very own life. It was a thought that was violently bothering me and I ended up asking it to her.

"There is another theory to it my dear which civilised gentlemen like you might not agree with... I am talking about marijuana or any other intoxicant for that matter.... For people like me, who know that there is hardly anything left in life, it does not require them to seek completeness. For them nothingness and emptiness also mean as important as completeness. And if you trust me, intoxication can also lead to enlightenment and grant the same happiness that you would otherwise seek through attaining completeness!"

Seeing Maya getting into the same old loop, I realised that she had reached the point of no return. Concurring with her theory of *listening to the soul*, I concluded that she was one of those brilliant human beings who never listened to her soul and wasted her valuable life chasing unreal and fragile happiness....

Enough was just enough and I decided to run off. It was two o'clock in the night, yet I called up Sreejith to pick me up from Maya's place.

Maya looked apparently dejected; though she didn't at all resist my decision to leave. I told her that the time I spent with her was special and thanked her rather soul fully for sharing her thoughts on *completeness of life* and *listening to the soul*. She smiled beautifully in acknowledgement and quickly grabbed the phone from my pocket and started inserting her numbers into my phonebook. She took my numbers and promised to call me once I reached India. I hugged her droopily and left without more ado.

I stayed almost awake the whole night at Sreejith's apartment recalling Maya's awe-inspiring theories. But more radically it was the paradox of *preaching-and-practicing* that kept me perplexed and amused....

When I woke up in the morning, I found myself lying on the floor with my head placed placidly between my bathroom slippers. I got up and looked around for Sreejith... I wanted him to help me with my return tickets....

"But *bhaiyya*, what about your plans...? You had told me that you would be going to see your friends in Boston and Baltimore? Wouldn't you be going now?"

I made a bit of confession to Sreejith... I told him that the *rage* which made me *run* this far had eventually evaporated following my exposure to a new found meaning of life and its completeness and hence, the urge to *prove* my worth did not subsist any more! I also admitted that my resolution to pursue a Ph.D. was a mere manifestation of my *rage* and *not* the call of my soul.

Sreejith looked all puzzled but I didn't bother to explain things further.

The next morning at seven, I was at the Amtrak Station waiting to catch The Saluki back to Chicago. Baba Menon, Sreejith and Maya had also joined in to see me off. We were all standing near the Snack Bar.... There was a weird silence surrounding us and none of us felt the itch to break it. We just continued looking at each other and all three of them kept making gestures that only I could read. There was a tired strain on Maya's face, Baba was still wearing his half-smile and Sreejith was just too lost about the way things happened!

The Saluki left Carbondale at 7:30; and so did I.

My flight from Chicago to London was at 5:30 in the evening and having reached Chicago at one o'clock, I decided not to see any of my friends there and instead rushed straightaway to the airport.

I ate lunch at one of the middling snack counters at Terminal 5 and dozed off as soon as I boarded the craft. I woke up an hour later and could not sleep for the rest of the night. I was thinking about Maya... I kept wondering.... How could this happen to her? She was too intelligent to get into what now seemed nothing less than a desperate suicidal trap.... Similar thoughts started popping out of my mind as I remembered my friend, Baba Menon. He was highly educated.... Yes, what else would you call him after having learnt that he was a graduate from IIT-Bombay and *almost* a doctorate in Bio Medical Engineering? Nonetheless, what I really liked about him was his blissful wisdom, which was just about unquestionable. But even with all my admiration for him, it was just impossible to ignore the way he too was heading for embracing a life of darkness and despair….

People like Baba and Maya could not be foolish... then were they too evolved? Were their pursuits beyond what I could appreciate? I was puzzled and sad….

My sadness seemed excruciating and it started growing implausibly intense when I realised that I didn't anymore have a goal in life to chase…. Maya was my only benchmark.... In fact, ever since the day in Delhi I felt betrayed at her hands, I was being solely driven by the conviction that my only purpose in life was to prove my *real* worth to her and get elevated to a new plane of self-pride that could free me from all inhibitions and let me pursue a life of passion. But contrary to my expectations, when I found Maya submerged in her disgraceful present and a predictably contemptible future, the whole purpose of my life began to seem misplaced. I wished I wouldn't have come to the US... I wished I never had discovered Maya's whereabouts. I wondered if things would have been brighter had Maya been a little better off. I cursed myself for all the years that I wasted *running with rage*. I felt terrible at realising how immature I was to believe that *winning over* somebody could grant me my life of passion. I blamed every thought and action of mine that drifted me away from my real self and pushed me into becoming a puppet of my resentful imaginations.

The pensiveness continued for a while…. But then, a throng of crude uncanny thoughts bubbled and spilled over and all of a sudden things started making miraculous sense to me…. All at once I got appallingly astonished at the imperceptible hand of destiny behind everything that I experienced over the last few weeks. Right from my decision to visit Doom Dooma; my coincidental rendezvous with Porrie; Sreejith and Maya being in the same town; Porrie speaking about Sreejith; to my subsequent trip to the US; everything seemed just too impossible to be a mere coincidence! I began to appreciate that it was my destiny that brought me back to Maya and presented me with the most enlightening moments of my life in the guise of unpleasant surprises and surprising revelations. I was further convinced that it was destiny that spoke through Baba and Maya to help me understand that life was not about running and proving...I felt like a child marvelled at the new discovery as I began seeing a purpose behind everything that I had gone through. I started discovering that destiny wanted me to appreciate that success is immaterial if it does not lead to *completeness*. I learnt that envy, pride and greed, which often push you to *run with rage*, might help you achieve relative material success but attaining *completeness and true happiness*, which is absolute, is all about *listening to your soul* and endeavouring to achieve its genuine wants. I also realised that being honest to one's own *soul* was far more important than *proving one's worth* to the world.

I felt relieved. I sighed in peace and asked for a can of beer. The beer arrived; I pop-opened it and began pouring it in the plastic glass that came along. I watched the sparkling golden liquid gradually filling the glass and I faintly asked myself if what I had been calling so was destiny indeed... I dwelled on it further and vaguely concluded that it could also be the thrust of the *soul*....

Within minutes, we arrived at London's Heathrow Airport. The time was seven o'clock in the morning.

Almost an hour later, I was at the coffee shop at Terminal 4; munching a ham-sandwich and listening to some old favourites on my tiny little MP3 player. I was relishing both... but suddenly, there was some noise and I felt a little bothered. I turned my ears and heard a lady arguing with the man in the shop. The lady sounded like an Indian. I ignored and continued munching. The fight stopped a while after.... There was silence and I was back to my relaxed-self. Unexpectedly, I heard the voice again. Amazingly, this time it sounded somewhat familiar too. I turned my head to see a lady in yellow *salwaar-kameez*. I stood up and walked a little closer to see if my guess was right.... That was almost she! ...Short, somewhat plump, fairish, square-jawed, thick-but-short-haired and evidently north Indian! But she looked quite young... almost a teenager.... How could she look so young? It has been more than fourteen years...!

I got puzzled and came back to grab the stool I was sitting on. The lady ogled at me for a second and started coming closer. I was nervous... I didn't react.

"Sidddhhaaaaaaarthaaaaaaa...!"

God! It was Dolly! Unbelievable! She looked just the same...! Even the yellow she was wearing seemed strikingly close to the *famous* mango-yellow sweater of her college days! I was just too excited... and simply couldn't believe my eyes.... Dolly drew herself a little closer and looked into my eyes. There was a bright cheerful smile on her face and her eyes were twinkling in joy. She was constantly lifting her arms and pulling them back at the same time. It seemed she wanted to hug me but resisted doing so for reasons that both of us could appreciate.

"Here I caught you, Siddhartha...! ...Where Siddhartha... where were you all this while? It has really been so many years... Siddhartha, you never responded to my letters! Why Siddhartha...? I wrote so many of them. Well that was ages back but now, around a year back, I had found you on a social networking website. I had sent you a message. But I guess you never bothered to respond. Never mind, now that I have caught you, it would be impossible for you to escape.... And where is my friend Aparoopa? Are you guys married to each other? Hey, I am sorry.... It was just a guess! It's absolutely okay if you are not! So where are you travelling to? Do you live in London?"

I looked at Dolly once again and noticed the only visible change in her.... She was wearing a *mangal-sutra*. I looked at her again and started responding to her queries one by one. I told her that I was on an official trip to the US and was on my way back to Pune, where I had been living ever since we lost touch with each other. I told her that her guess about Aparoopa being married to me was correct.... Thrilled and stunned, she jumped thrice in apparent joy, clapping her hands like a colourful toy clown!

"*Actually,* mine is a long story; but don't worry, I wouldn't make it sound so long!"

Dolly still sounded like a youngster.... From the excitement on her face it was evident that she was about to come up with something that she believed to be extraordinarily eventful and truly one of its kind. But honestly, I was not in the kind of mood to listen to yet another dramatic tale. I was just too tired of listening. I wanted to rest. But having realised that I couldn't have thought of another way to pass my time at the airport, I let Dolly go ahead.

"Remember, I used to teach in a school in Mussoorie? *Actually*, in one of the winters, I had come to Dehradun to spend the holidays with my parents.... An old friend of my father, who had migrated to the UK years ago, was in town. He was on a bride-hunt for his one and only son, and had spotted one *Khatri* gentleman in our locality who had two college-going daughters in his family. Things were almost final.... Now both the families just wanted Rajesh, the groom, to come down from London and make his choice between the two women. Rajesh came, visited the family, met and rejected both the girls and was almost on his way back to London. My parents invited Rajesh and his father for dinner and in our very first meeting, Rajesh and I sensed a wonderful compatibility between us.... Towards the end of the same evening, together we decided to approach our respective parents for their consent! We weren't too sure about them because Rajesh wasn't a *Rajput* and right from my school days my parents had made it pretty clear that I wouldn't be allowed to marry anybody outside the community... I was anxious but Rajesh was calm and composed. He was far more matured and wise. After all he was a neurosurgeon... Dr. Rajesh Khanna! The next day, Rajesh came home with his father and spent the afternoon convincing my parents. Finally, my father agreed on the condition that we would have a *Rajput* wedding, to which the father and the son instantly agreed and within hours, at 2 a.m., we had our ring ceremony.... Three months later, we got married! Interesting, isn't it?"

Boring! Typical *Bollywood style love-cum-arranged* wedding stories! I just wished that was the end of it.... But Dolly looked all excited... I guessed her story had not ended... I was right!

"So for the last eight years, we have been living here in London. It's a nice place. But mind you, it is horrifically expensive too! In fact, everything here is just too pricey! *Actually*, even the normal life here is kind of weird. We don't go out. We don't meet people. *Actually*, calling people home and hosting parties can be an extremely costly affair! Anyway, we don't even have too many friends. So why worry about parties.... You know, at times I feel absolutely cut off from the world. And to tell you the truth, I have always been trying to influence Rajesh about going back to India and find some work there. Just enough of London now...! We have earned enough, seen enough. Now I wish we settle down in any of the nicer cities in India, have a proper family and just live a decent social life... Bangalore...! That's one good place! In fact, in the past ten months I have been frequenting to that city to set up a small non-profit organisation called *Disha*. *Actually*, from my early childhood, I had treasured the dream of working for the cause of *women's education* and through *Disha* I have been able to live that dream. I am in the process of setting up two project offices; one each in Bangalore and Ahmedabad. Our plan is to get non-profits registered with us. These would be the ones with FCRA registration, that is, non-profits who are allowed to receive foreign funds. I have a network of volunteers in US and UK who would help us with the fund-raising and the funds thus raised shall be extended to the registered non-profits to support the cause. Believe me Siddhartha; I am just too excited about this project! But somehow I feel my husband is not very keen. He has never been unaccommodating though.... But I wanted him to join me in this mission. He could have easily started a charitable hospital or anything that makes sense to him... God knows what that man is up to...!"

It was 10:20; time to board the craft... I slowly got up and started walking towards the boarding queue. Dolly hurried to the airline's enquiry counter to check something about her baggage. While I was in the queue, I saw her coming back to join in. But by the time I was in the craft, she was lost.

We reached Mumbai at 00:15 in the night. I was standing in the long queue for Customs Clearance, when I saw Dolly approaching. I came out of the line and waved at her. She parked her baggage trolley beside and told me that she was on her way to the domestic airport as she planned to catch the early morning flight to Bangalore. We exchanged phone numbers and promised not to lose touch again. Dolly hinted that she might come to Pune for some *evaluation work* in the coming months and I extended a polite invitation in response. We passed the Customs, walked up to the cabs together and parted like mere acquaintances.

9

Song of the Soul

I switched on my mobile phone and asked the cab driver to stop as we approached Khandala. Probably, I had sensed that my drained self was not quite prepared to face Aparoopa... I felt I needed to give myself a little more time....

I lit a cigarette, looked all around and instead of taking the straight road to Pune, asked the driver to get off the expressway and guided him to a friend's place near Khandala Bazaar. Rocky Kanjani....My only bachelor friend; a door that I could knock at any hour of the night; the only condition being a drink or two or three or four...!

"Siddie; you devil! ...at three o'clock in the night? Come on in, *bastard*! ... *Kya hua*...? Everything's okay *na*?"

I told Rocky that I was coming back from a conference in Mumbai and as Aparoopa was also not at home, I thought of waking him up for a drink. He didn't bother to know more and plainly got a bottle of whisky, some ice-cubes and two glasses.

It was always a pleasure to watch Rocky uncorking the bottle....

Rocky started making the drink as I shared some of my *duty-free shopping* with him saying that a colleague of mine whom I met in Mumbai had just been back from the US and got those presents for me. Rocky didn't bother to look at it but somehow also didn't miss to spot the pack of his favourite Benson & Hedges cigarettes. He picked it up, opened it and lit a cigarette with his ever-favourite five-rupee-lighter.

"Buddy, if there's any serious trouble, you can stay at my place as long as you want. I am sorry if I have made you feel uncomfortable by saying this but in the last eight years there hasn't been a single occasion when you and Aparoopa haven't been together. Whatever it is, till you sort it out, just feel free to stay here, okay?"

I had no intentions of staying with Rocky for anything longer than the night. I just wanted to unwind myself from the hangover of the trip and gather my thoughts together before I go to Sapatnekar for seeking his help on my quest ahead.

I finished my drink and went asleep on the sofa. I woke up at around noon time and called up Sapatnekar. He was at his centre and asked me to join him there. We finished lunch by two o'clock and drove down to Sapatnekar's centre at Dehu Road. It didn't take us even twenty minutes to reach there on Rocky's ancient metallic-blue Maruti 800.

"Welcome back, *Sirjee*? So, how was it? How close are you now to your *pride* and *passion*?"

Sapatnekar's bewilderment saw no end when he learnt how far my self-quest had taken me beyond Doom Dooma!

"US...? Are you kidding me? Why and what for?"

It took me almost the entire evening to narrate the whole story; right from my meeting with Porrie at the bar in Doom Dooma up to my rediscovery of Maya, her present state, the people around her, their theories... *running with rage*, *completeness* and *listening to the soul* and the paradox of *preaching-and-practising!*

Sapatnekar looked amused but not at all surprised.... As if he knew everything beforehand... He didn't speak much and just let me go on with my saga. And as I finished, he took a deep breath and smiled at me with his mischievous wink.

"Today, I am really very happy for you Siddhartha! In fact I am equally happy for myself...! In the last twenty-two years, as a practitioner, I have seen thousands of cases of *midlife-crisis* but yours turned out to be really unique! Do you know why? Hmmm... yours is the first case where I have actually seen the subject himself owning up the responsibility of finding the remedy! So far, in most of my cases, I have helped my clients to reach the root of their problems but finding a solution being extremely subjective, it required enormous effort on the clients' part and that's where everyone gave up! You are a brave guy Siddhartha. Just keep up this spirit of yours!"

Sapatnekar's abrupt excitement indistinctly surprised me but I nodded in acknowledgement to let him continue....

"Honestly my friend, I am really impressed with the way you have gone about your quest! And if you believe me, you are already there...."

"Your observation on the paradox of *preaching-and-practicing* is absolutely solid. You know Siddhartha; there are basically three categories of seekers in this world. The first; that does not listen to the soul and always seeks things that are either wrong or irrelevant... The second; that partially listens to the soul and recognises the right things but cannot or do not put the right effort to achieve them; and the third is the kind that is in complete harmony with the soul and thus identifies the right things, looks at them from the right perspective and puts effort in the right magnitude and direction to accomplish them! I have a strong sense that unlike the Mayas and the Babas of the world, you, by the virtue of your quest, have gradually moved into the third category and that gives me all the hope! Now coinciding with your newly discovered theories, which seem perfect to their core, I would like to see you getting over your *rage* and seeking *completeness* by unfailingly following your *soul....*"

I could appreciate everything that Sapatnekar was saying. I could then also make greater sense out of the philosophies that Baba and Maya preached. But somewhere in my heart of hearts, I had a doubt.... Somehow I felt that I was not too sure about what *listening to the soul* exactly meant... I wanted Sapatnekar to help me understand how and when one would know what the soul is trying to convey....

"Keep doing everything that you love doing! If you feel that you are doing it to prove yourself superior to someone or to live up to a challenge that somebody has thrown at you, you should recognise that it is not something that your soul is driving you to do. Just remember, whenever you feel that you are being driven by pride, prejudice, jealousy, greed etc., you should sense the alarm that you are defying your soul and drifting away from it. I am sure you are not alien to this feeling. In fact, the very reason that compelled you to turn away from your plan of doing a Ph.D. in the US lies in the fact that you obeyed your soul's verdict!"

There was amazing concurrence between Sapatnekar's reasoning and what I had interpreted from my practical experiences and my fanatical interactions with Baba and Maya. His gripping deliberation was constantly reinforcing my conviction and I was silently rejoicing over the fact that my trip to the US didn't go in vain!

"When you listen to your soul, you do what you really like doing and not what others have been successful with. Often, allured by the success of others, people end up doing things that do not naturally come to them.... In such situations, the only thing that is certain is failure! When you ape others, you focus more on your weaknesses; your efforts are always aimed at *correcting* yourself! And trust me, that's not necessary and more importantly, that's not how one achieves excellence. You attain excellence only when you focus on your strengths! How much ever you try, you can never be somebody else. Similarly you cannot excel in things that do not come naturally to you! When you listen to your soul, you stop aping others and do things that you genuinely love doing. Success and failure become simply immaterial. And that's exactly when you start living your life of passion!"

Sapatnekar was sounding more than just accurate! Never before in my life had I felt so tremendously convinced! Every passing moment, he was making astounding revelations that were rekindling the dormant spark in me....

"Siddhartha, I can bet on anything to prove that you are an absolute Romanticist.... Well, do you know what a Romanticist is? Hmmm... actually, Romanticism was a movement that had started in Europe in the later part of Eighteenth century.... It had brought about a significant importance to nature, emphasised on creative expression of emotions, and caused a massive upheaval against conventional social standards.... Well, now I called you a true Romanticist because throughout these years of our friendship, I have found you to be an exceptionally creative person. But it's rather sad that to date I have never seen you being serious about your creativity. Honestly, so far what I have seen in you is just the tendency... Siddhartha, I am yet to see the real action! And trust me my friend, if you want to live your life of passion, you must keep your creative spark alive! You must chase your creative pursuits with all your passion! That would energise your endeavours to accomplish completeness and self-actualization. And don't ever be misled; it is not at all necessary to become an ascetic and shun the material world to seek your creative passion. You can do that by living in the world that you have always been a part of! Career and family are extremely critical to completeness. So quitting your professional career or your family life is not advisable. You see Siddhartha, completeness or true happiness calls for accomplishments on multiple fronts and your professional career is a vital element to it.

Besides, the very fact that you have come this far in your career proves that you are worthy of it! You are probably among those top few percentage of people who have it in them to make it really big in their professional lives. So it would be great injustice to leave your career in the lurch! Live the life you deserve! Don't just quit and run! And of course, you must also understand that creative people enjoy the best of all the worlds... I mean, along with pursuing your creative passions you can also be creative in your job and family front as well. Try looking out for ways everyday to make your job more interesting! Invent creative ways of enjoying your family life more than ever before. That's how you would experience life to its fullest! And that's exactly what completeness is all about!"

I was thoroughly convinced... Sapatnekar's compelling philosophy sounded so encouraging that I felt motivated to go back to my usual life and start afresh with a refurbished drive.

It was getting dark and Sapatnekar was packing up for the day... I asked him if he could drop me somewhere in the city. He smiled and nodded and I rushed into his car without a further thought.

I was all excited.... I was going home after almost a month! I remembered Aparoopa and felt extremely guilty about my disappearing act.... I closed my eyes in repentance and promised myself of not repeating it ever....

It was a hot May evening. The expressway even at nine in the night looked parched and dead beat.... The setting inside Sapatnekar's SUV was however quite unlike.... The mildly cool air-conditioning, the old *Dev Anand* numbers playing in the background and Sapatnekar zooming fast ahead, whistling and singing along the tracks.... It indeed felt like a joyful home-coming!

We reached Pune and Sapatnekar dropped me home.

The walk from the approach to the stairs of the building where I lived seemed like a distance of miles. My heart was beating fast and I wasn't too sure if I would be able to face Aparoopa... I was nervous. I reached the stairs, climbed them under an unexplainable pressure and ultimately reached the door with a rather spine-chilling fear.... To my surprise, the door was locked! It was 10:30 p.m. and usually Aparoopa is home by that time. I got a little worried but decided to wait. I left my baggage at the door, went up to the benches at the common lawns and spent almost an hour sitting there, smoking a couple of cigarettes and trying to reach Aparoopa on her cell-phone. It was switched off !

At around 11:15, I saw a car coming.

It was dark outside but I could vaguely figure out that it was Mishra and his wife Vibha, our next door neighbours. But there was another person, evidently a lady, sitting at the rear seat.... It was Aparoopa. I got up quickly and started following the car through the parking. The car stopped and Vibha came out hastily to open the door for Aparoopa. I was confused. I rushed... and by the time I could reach there, Aparoopa had just managed to get out of the car with Vibha's support. Aparoopa looked frail and tired... I felt terribly miserable to see her in that state. I cursed myself for my negligent behaviour and turned to Mishra and Vibha to know what exactly had happened. Vibha gawked at me in an unreasonable anguish and spoke up in her rather boorish voice....

"At around nine o'clock, after coming back from work, we were generally chatting near the club-house and she started complaining of stomach ache and giddiness. Luckily, my husband was around and we took her to the hospital. But by the time we reached the hospital, she started feeling better and insisted that we come back. We waited for sometime and when she sounded absolutely confident, we went to Marzorin to have ice-cream. Having ice-cream at Marzorin, we came back! Good that you are back!" She ended abruptly with a hint of sarcasm.

I looked at Apu and just couldn't control the tears that rolled shamelessly down my cheeks. I tried holding her by her arms but she softly pulled herself away. I knew that she hated me.... She had every right and reason....

Vibha helped Apu climb the stairs up to the lift and I quietly followed the two ladies. Aparoopa opened the door and we went inside. In a deep sense of annoyance I threw myself at the sofa and wept for minutes like a helpless child. Apu was unmoved though. She went to the kitchen, got herself a bottle of water from the fridge, went into the bedroom and latched it from inside.... I spent the whole night waiting for her in the living room....

Almost towards the crack of dawn, I heard Apu opening the door. I was too scared to react and remained composed on the sofa. I heard her coming towards me.... And almost abruptly, I felt a hit on my belly. Even before I could respond, I felt a hard slap on my left cheek which was rapidly followed by two more on the other. I looked at Apu. She was howling. She was in pain. She didn't have words to express her fury. She looked just too distressed. I tried hugging her but she resisted. She was shivering in wrath. She was still sobbing... Trying to comfort her, I pulled her into my arms and looked into her eyes.... They didn't demand any apology. They didn't seek any explanation. They were just tired... tired of seeing my recklessness over and again....

I felt trounced by guilt and repentance and I remained quiet. I stood up, went to the kitchen and made two cups of tea. We sat at the balcony and slowly sipped off our tea. Finally, Aparoopa spoke up.

"So what have you decided, Siddhartha?"

Aparoopa sounded grave and reticent; as if she wanted to understand from me for one last time... I didn't know what exactly she wanted me to tell her. However, I attempted... I attempted answering her question with all my earnestness. I didn't lie. I didn't cook up stories. I didn't beat around the bush. I just told Aparoopa the truth. I told her that all this while I was chasing a mirage. I told her that the Maya I had been unthinkingly contending with didn't really exist. I told her about my visit to the US and shared everything that I learnt about Maya and my own self upon meeting her there. I assured Aparoopa that though I had travelled all the way to the US just to get a closer glimpse into Maya's present life, I genuinely had no intentions of wooing her or getting her back in to my life. I made a huge effort to let Aparoopa know that my struggle to prove my worth to Maya was actually my deep aspiration of achieving my own potential. I told her that the sheer absence of a meaningful goal in my life had compelled me to seek an external anchor, which for known and unknown reasons assumed the guise of Maya and that pushed me on and on towards an untamed rage which forced my bamboozled self run eccentrically to prove its *worth*.

"But how will things be different now?"

I expound my discovery to Aparoopa that the life of passion I had endlessly been chasing is not about ascertaining one's pride or proving one's worth. It is rather far more internal to the self and intertwined with the soul... Assuring her that henceforth every endeavour of mine would be focused on looking inward and listening to the soul, I promised her that I would never have to break away from her to live my life of passion!

Aparoopa's eyes didn't really throw any hint of disbelief. But she didn't seem entirely convinced either.

"Well, I have to go to work now. I will see you in the evening. There are some noodles in the fridge. You can have it for lunch if you wish...."

Aparoopa left for work and I began working on my plan for the day. It all seemed like a new beginning.... Following Sapatnekar's advice, I tried to be as creative as possible....

To start with, I went to the nearby superstore to buy broccoli, capsicum, tomatoes, basil-leaves, ginger, coconut-milk and of course tiger-prawns; the ingredients for Apu's favourite Burmese Prawns Curry! I came home, prepared the curry and cooked some Coriander Rice. Next, I called up Aparoopa, told her that there was some surprise for her and drove up to her office and got her home for lunch.

Aparoopa looked amazed and visibly delighted, though she didn't express it in so many words.

We finished lunch and I went to drop Aparoopa back at her office. The next item on my agenda was to call up my boss, Kalra. I kept trying his number but his phone remained constantly engaged. I gave up, stopped at a *pan* kiosk to lit my cigarette and my phone rang. It was Kalra....

"Hey... Siddhartha! Sorry; I was on a call with a prospective partner in Thailand... Tell me buddy, how's your sabbatical treating you? Do you really have any plans of coming back to us? Hahaha... hey just kidding, buddy!"

I decided to sound uncomplicated. So without giving him any further chance to crack his usual foul jokes, I told him straightaway that I had dropped my sabbatical plans and was willing to join back within a month's time.

Kalra took a while to respond. Probably there was some calculation going on in his mind. It seemed that he was just about to propose some alternative....

"What if I ask you to join next week? Actually, I would want you to go to Thailand and work with the new partner there for a month or so. In fact, till the moment you called, I was thinking of Ninad for this job but somehow I wasn't too comfortable.... It would be good Siddhartha if you resume work next week... Look buddy, I know that you have been for long looking at taking up an international assignment and now that the opportunity has actually come in, wouldn't it be unwise on your part to turn it down?"

Kalra was probably right. It might have been unwise to turn down the offer. I didn't think much... I politely conveyed my acceptance and Kalra asked me to see him sometime in the next week.

"Wow! That's cool, Sid! So finally my hubby's going on an international assignment! I am really so happy, Sid! ...I wish once you come back from Thailand, they'll be further convinced of your capabilities and reconsider their decision of sending you permanently to Australia!"

Apu sounded excited. But she looked sad as well. Probably she didn't want us to part again... Nor did I....

I wanted to be at home. It was important for me to be with Apu. It was needed that I focus on my new learning and practice it. After all, I had to work towards my life of passion! But I was confused... I was not being able to make my choice....

I had a week's time in my hand and those seven days meant a lot to me. Regardless of what I would finally decide to opt for, I was convincingly certain about one thing; that I would spend every minute of the week re-dedicating myself to my commitment of being creative about every action of mine in every sphere of my life. This conviction filled my heart with a renewed optimism and provoked me to accept Kalra's proposal in a new spirit and outlook.

I confirmed my consent to Kalra and assured him of my resumption from the fifteenth of May. Kalra was impressed with my *energy* and he initiated the visa application process without losing any time.

The days I spent with Aparoopa till I left for Thailand turned out to be some of the most cheerful times of my adult life.... As I gradually disclosed the crux of my new-found revelations to her, I saw her believably joining and supporting me on every attempt of mine to pursue them. Rising well ahead of sunrise, walking miles from home to behold the rising sun over the Kanifnath Caves, teaching a rhyme to the village children on the way, clicking pictures of wild berries and flowers, humming a few lines from some old romantic numbers, driving down to the villages nearby to buy farm fresh fruits and vegetables and cooking a wholesome traditional afternoon meal at home; everything that I experienced in those amazing days filled my heart with a deep sense of fulfilment. I began to discover that with a mere stroke of creative contentment, I could appreciate the new promises—the small, the big and the untold, that every day dawned with! I also began to sense the endless *oomph of a thousand suns* that each of these promises brought with it! It felt almost like childhood and I was instinctively inspired to live every moment of it. Surprisingly, those magical moments of peace and happiness never really drifted me apart from my *practical* responsibilities.

Although, I had not officially resumed work, everyday I made it a point to spend time with Kalra on the phone to try and understand the company's plans in Thailand. I spent the late evenings reading *white-papers* and *analyst reports* on the Banking Industry in Thailand and browsing through some of the relevant literature on the web. I studied the complete assessment report that Ninad had prepared on *TechBank Solutions,* the prospective partner and also worked on the *portfolio of services* that we could jointly offer to the Thai Banks. Amusingly, even before Kalra could ask for it, I was already set with my complete business strategy.

On the night of the first of June, I left for Thailand. The next morning at five, I was at the Suvarnabhumi International Airport, Bangkok. Khun Sarawut, the CEO of TechBank Solutions himself was present at the airport to receive me. Polite, smiling and modestly witty, he appeared to be more than just a 'pleasure to work with'!

Khun Sarawut dropped me at a modestly decent hotel off Petchburi Road near the famous Pratunam Market and headed off for his office which was just a ten-minute's drive from the hotel. He allowed me the first half of the day to freshen up and get over my exhaustion as he promised to pick me up at two in the afternoon.

Sharp at 2, Khun Sarawut was at my door, knocking.

Presuming that being a Hindu I ought to be a pure vegetarian, he took me to an Indian restaurant famous for its extensive varieties of *dals*, *rotis*, and *paneer* preparations. I felt out of place and upon confirming that he had not reserved any table in our name, I spent no time and ran out frantically to grab and savour some of the celebrated street food of Bangkok.

Moo, that's pork, stewed with assorted vegetables and served with hot steamed rice and ice tea...! That was my first meal in Bangkok at a grimy-trifling-stinky street side food cart! It was just *too* good!

I sensed that I was being quite a shock to Khun Sarawut.... But he was not the one to have explicitly expressed his reactions.... He maintained his wise inertness and kept smiling at me as I hogged on sitting on a creaky old aluminium stool at the stinky street-side eatery.

After that lovely maiden Thai meal, Khun Sarawut and I proceeded to the office of TechBank Solutions at Soi 31 off Sukhumvit Road.

TechBank Solutions operated from a small *serviced office* with around twenty work-stations and two meeting rooms; one small and one relatively larger. Khun Sarawut mentioned that he mostly worked out of the smaller meeting room, which staged a sizeably large glass window that offered the best possible view of the city!

I stood at the window and stretched my sight over the spectacular view....

It seemed as if the entire city of Bangkok was under my eyes! Lucky Sarawut; it was such a privilege to be on the fifteenth floor of the majestic Golden Towers!

"Come, let's do some work now! All play and no work in Bangkok will definitely make Khun Siddhartha a very naughty boy!"

Khun Sarawut meant business. For the time-being, he didn't seem to allow much time for observations and polite conversations.

I felt coerced to take out my laptop and started making my presentations to the team present without being introduced appropriately.

Glancing over the faces around, I figured out that it was an all-Thai group. Language, however, didn't really play much of a barrier as most of them understood and spoke English.

Surprisingly, one of the team members, a lady, spoke in an accent rather close to that of my friends in the US.... All throughout the afternoon her noticeably dissimilar mannerism kept stealing all my attention. But in spite of constant distractions, I managed to complete my two-hour long presentation keeping everyone reasonably engaged as I took the team through our company profile, the global clientele, our policies on partnership and alliances and the potential market in Thailand for our joint and bundled offerings.

"Khun Siddhartha, this is Sukhon, our Marketing Communications person..." introduced Khun Sarawut pointing his hand at the same lady who amazed me with her surprisingly American mannerisms and diction. "She and our Sales Head, Alex, would be your local guides... I have asked both of them to take good care of yours and take you around Bangkok in your leisure time. In fact, Sukhon lives very close to Pratunam, the place where your hotel is… if you are interested, she will show you some of the temples and palaces that Bangkok is famous for! Mind you, most of our temples are not open after six in the evening so if you can wake up early, you can see them in the morning before we start work. And yes; not to forget; do push Sukhon upon inviting you to her place for dinner! That's an opportunity you cannot afford to miss… Khun Siddhartha, I bet you wouldn't find a better cook elsewhere in Bangkok!

I spent twenty one days in Bangkok working with Alex on the sales-pipeline, with Sukhon on the marketing collaterals and with Khun Sarawut on the overall strategies and agreements. I spent the early mornings visiting temples with Sukhon, learning more about the Thai heritage and culture and making new discoveries everyday about the great wisdom of Theravada Buddhism and the eternal power of Buddhist meditation and contemplation. The evenings however looked different… Nightclubs, hostess bars, massage parlours and wherever else Alex took me to…. It was a life of contrasts; and gradually, I was adapting to appreciate the divergence. However, as the days progressed, I increasingly found myself spending more time with Sukhon; visiting places, appreciating the world around and appreciating her all the more.

In one of those radiant mornings, in the beautiful premises of the Wat Phra Kaew, the Temple of the Emerald Buddha, as I watched my young urban smart intelligent good-looking guide Sukhon soulfully closing her eyes and bowing to the Great Master, I discovered in her the rare embodiment of the eternal completeness that the great spiritual scriptures of the world merely mentioned of ! In her, I witnessed for the first ever time the convergence of the contrasts, the confluence of matter and spirit, the union of the ordinary and the divine and the oneness of sexuality and spirituality. In that woman, I saw the young and attractive Sukhon who of late had convincingly become the object of my astounding desire and I also saw in the same woman, the Sukhon who uncompromisingly commanded my reflective admiration for being the symbol of angelic serenity. For all intents and purposes, I concluded that it was the expression and the transcendence of the divine unity over man's duality; a yet another testimony to the existence of the *One Great Soul* that lives through every minute particle of the unending universe!

My sojourn at the flamboyant-yet-spiritual Bangkok and the mesmerizsing presence of Sukhon inadvertently drove me into a gleaming new realm of consciousness. The *oomph of the thousand suns* was evolving further... I began to discover that every aspect of life, good or bad; every object in the universe, vast or minute and every emotion, positive or negative, had its own relevance in the greater scheme of things.

On the last day of work at Khun Sarawut's office, as I stood once again in front of the glass window to catch the last few glimpses of the city that I had lately fallen in love with and witnessed it getting merrily drenched in the first showers of the south-west monsoons, my *soul* cried in awe of the *completeness* that every moment of divinity had resplendently reproduced... I gazed at the vastness of the rains and remembered the enormity of the Reclining Buddha at Wat Phra Chetuphon. I quietly smiled at the triviality of man's existence without the consciousness of the *Great Soul*.

All of a sudden, the long-famished dormant poet dying deep within me impulsively bloomed into a buoyant resurrection to resonate the *song* of my *soul* in appreciation of the magnificence of the *soul of the universe*. It sang about the world. It sang about nature. It sang about mankind. It sang about the childhood joys and the agonies of adult life.... It sang about the perfect dreams and the illusions that misguide them! It sang and just sang till suddenly, there was a pause as I heard somebody approaching from behind. It was Sukhon. I turned back and looked at her and then into her tranquil eyes... They were beautiful as the rains. They were profound as the holy chants. They were sparkling with the divine rhythm of eternity; the rhythm that at last made my song complete; the rhythm that stirred up my *soul* to go on....

10

And It Led My Way!

"CONGRATULATIONS, my tiger! You did it! Khun Sarawut just now spoke with me on the phone. He seems to be very impressed about the way you guided his team. Good job Siddhartha and keep it up! So by what time would you be reaching Mumbai?"

Kalra didn't really wait for my response and started talking to somebody else on the other phone. He wasn't bothered… Neither was I!

I reached Mumbai at 10:00 p.m. The four and half hours on the flight passed apparently like a twenty-minute nap. But I was not sleeping… I was awake; astonished and overwhelmed by the unbroken thoughts about the incredible journey that my soul artfully made me undertake through an unanticipated assortment of explicit and implicit pretexts.

As I checked out of the Mumbai Airport and hurried towards the cabs, I reflected further and began realising the greater meaning hidden behind the sequence of events that first led me to recognize the very existence of my soul, then prompted and inspired me to listen to it and then finally gifted me with the consciousness about the soul of the universe. It felt elating. It sounded like a tryst with what the world knows by the name of God! All of a sudden, every moment of the journey; every person whom I met in the course of it, every incident that I experienced as a part of it, and every lesson that I learnt appeared to be an outcome of a deliberate divine intervention. Ninad, Porrie, Dr. Sapatnekar, Maya, Baba Menon, Sukhon and every other person who at some stage of my journey consciously or unconsciously led me further in my quest started appearing nothing less than the discernible manifestation of the *Great Soul*....

I closed my eyes in deep contemplation, thanked each one of them and felt the uncompromising urge to let my soul sing aloud its song in the praise of the *Great Soul*. It sang and I sang along....

"Honey...! I have some news for you. I bet you wouldn't believe it! Hey, no, don't be scared!!! No honey, it's some good news.... In fact, it's very good news! Just close your eyes and let me whisper it to you...."

I had absolutely no clue about what Apu was up to but I still followed her instructions, closed my eyes and waited for her to whisper...

"Daddy...! Hello Daddy...! ...Did you hear that honey?"

I was still clueless and blank... Apu gave me a rather animated stare to express her disgust and I sensed that she was indeed talking about something exceptionally significant... I had almost guessed *it* when she impatiently spelt it out....

"Idiot, you are going to be a father!"

I couldn't believe my ears... After so many years of our marriage, after so many years of childlessness and after so many years of utter despair, my ears had grown abhorrently pessimistic. They had just ceased to expect...

"You remember I was not feeling well for sometime... . So yesterday I went to the gynecologist for a general check-up and she by some means suspected a pregnancy. She asked me to get a few tests done and this afternoon she finally confirmed... Can you believe it, honey? Isn't it amazing? Well, you wouldn't be able to see the bulge but the doctor said I am already in the tenth week.... Well, it has to be! I wish I had known it much earlier that you need a hit on the head to get going.... We would have been proud parents of a school-going kid by now. Never mind, all's well that ends well! ...But you are happy *na*, honey?"

My heart was beating like a hurtling wild horse. I was experiencing a thrill that was never mine any time before! I felt like running, jumping, dancing and screaming. Deep within, I experienced oceans of emotions burbling and roaring.... The throbbing void in me that I had been deliberately disregarding so far made its hard presence felt as it primed to make way for its own desertion. I felt the welcoming gush of a new time. It was like a feeling of *completeness*. It sensed like the beginning of an evolving bond with the coming times.... My soul echoed my incomprehensible joy as it resumed its mystic song recounting the significance of the obligation that man fulfils by extending new life to nature to become an eternal entity.

The next morning dawned with a new eagerness. Aparoopa's growingly radiant face was glowing with an effervescent joy blended with a sense of subtle pride! She looked beautiful and complete. For a moment I felt as if all my recent discoveries and learning meant nothing against the tinkling pleasure that our so far elusive parenthood had finally brought into our lives... I mulled over the feeling for a while but steadily appreciated that I still needed to live my life of passion in order to righteously fulfil the demands of competent fatherhood. I wanted to validate the realism of my thoughts and decided to call Dr. Sapatnekar....

"Wonderful! This is a treasure! You can't afford to lose it, Siddhartha! This is exactly what listening to your soul means. I always knew that you were very close to it but wasn't too sure that you would find it so soon! Just a caution my friend.... The world around is too attractive and influential. You would tend to get carried away by all sorts of distractions and all the hard slog behind your quest and revelations would just go waste. So till your discoveries are still fresh in your mind, just ensure that you make a note of them. You can write them the way you like but I would strongly recommend that you narrate them in the form of your experiences in the sequence of chronology. That would help you even in the future to relate your theories to specific positions and circumstances! And yes, don't forget the song of your soul. In fact, that is what is going to be your polestar. Just be guided by that!"

Dr. Sapatnekar's inputs came in as a burly confidence-booster and I started off impatiently writing a quick passage describing flashes from the early phases of my self-quest.... And that was the spark which kindled the wild fire within me.

It was enlivening to behold my own-self being led by my soul towards my life of passion. It seemed as if every additional word and every advancing page propelled me to the fore on my journey towards completeness. As I recalled my experiences and revealed the secrets of life that I had fondly embarked upon, I relived an inexplicable catharsis that freed me from the pangs of my past and energized my soul to lead me further. And then there was no looking back.

Every evening after coming back from work, I diligently spent hours on my laptop capturing my thoughts and experiences in the exact chronology, further explicating and exemplifying them to help myself understand and analyse them better.

Soon, my expressions started assuming the silhouette of a tale, in the early course of which, I recalled and re-assessed the concept of *midlife-crisis* and revealed the hidden opportunity that every crisis treasures in its heart, the key to it being man's sheer ability to unleash the power of his soul to endure and transcend it. I mulled over my thoughts further on to reaffirm that across civilisations spanning centuries, for those led by their souls, *midlife-crisis* has insistently been the catalyst for generating the beginning of a more meaningful life and hence it rather deserved to be called *midlife-morphosis*.

Of late, my tale was evolving to conquer the potential of a book, which I quietly wished to call *The Midlife Morphosis*....

Working on *The Midlife Morphosis,* I discovered myself being miraculously possessed by the resolute influence of some divine intoxication that drove my senses to live my ultimate passion, the quest for which had so far been the sole purpose of my sheer existence.

For the first ever time, I was feeling so involved and driven.... There was so much that I wanted to express. There was so much that I wanted to write.... And amazingly, every time I sat down to accomplish that, I sensed a profoundly powerful propulsion, which I assumed to be that of the *Great Soul*, invigorating my expressions; so much so that in countless instances, I could tangibly feel that I was just being a medium! Humbly, I accepted the divine subjugation and blissfully witnessed and celebrated the emergence of my life of passion with the convergence of my *soul* into the *soul of the universe*.

Material success, power, pride, greed, envy and prejudice, all vanished into the precinct of non-existence. My soul was at peace and my heart breathed bliss. I experienced a life that was enormously more ecstatic than the soothing effect of alcohol or the superlative experience of a perfect orgasm. Every moment that I passionately dedicated to express my soul seemed perfectly complete and I felt phenomenally energised to write on for days together.... Twenty-seven consecutive days, rather nights, to be precise... Yet I didn't experience a moment of fatigue. Rather, the feeling was that of inexhaustible youthfulness and intense rejuvenation.... With an escalating consciousness about my own-self, I began appreciating the relevance of each and every experience of mine from the past, ever since the days of childhood, in the greater scheme of things that defined the journey of my soul. Every aspiration, every decision, every success, every failure, every tryst, every departure, every gain, every loss, every like, every dislike, every desire, every sacrifice, every gain and every loss seemed to be just another step towards accomplishing the journey of my soul and embracing a life of passion! Soon I realised that failure, loss, pain and regret were mere manifestations of the divine motivation for man to move on and attain completeness and true happiness... I also understood that the only secret to a complete and a meaningful life is to live every moment of it with utmost passion and genuine purpose, as every given moment is incredibly complete in itself when viewed against the backdrop of eternity!

The dire need to let the volcano of my effusive expressions erupt, almost unknowingly, turned me into a passionate story teller. In just twenty seven nights, the anecdotal illustrations of my life's experiences and revelations assumed the form of a thick bundle of two hundred odd pages that I, on being advised by Dr. Sapatnekar, sent to a few publishing houses for editorial assessment.

"Siddhartha, don't be foolish! You don't know what you have struck upon. No publisher in this world would ever want to miss the opportunity of printing such a magnificent piece of authentic soul searching experience. Just go ahead and mail your samples to all the major publishers...."

Dr. Sapatnekar was too optimistic. I too was somewhat convinced. I ended up following his advice.

"But Siddhartha, just help me understand; how did you manage to finish your book in such a short time. Had you taken a break from work or something? Or you managed to work on it even while you were at work?"

Dr. Sapatnekar was not convinced. He couldn't believe that by spending merely four hours every evening one could finish writing a book over just twenty seven days. He, being a reasonably prolific writer himself, was pretty much aware that it was just not possible! His probe therefore continued... He knew that I was not lying but he was not satisfied with my answers either.

Almost a week later, Dr. Sapatnekar invited me to his centre at Dehu Road. Although it was late afternoon, the skies were turning steadily dark. Monsoons were at their peak and the chilly breeze across the foothills was throwing its usual enigmatic charm. Dr. Sapatnekar at the outhouse of his centre was waiting for me to join him for his evening drink. The flavour of the evening was some Irish whisky!

"My friend; yours is not an ordinary story! No, I am not talking about your book. I am talking about the speed at which you managed to complete writing it. Siddhartha, I wouldn't ask you any further questions... I believe I have figured out my answer.... It is your soul! And now that you are in complete alignment with your soul, you will find your way ahead. Completeness or true happiness is now your destiny. And now it is almost irrevocable; provided you keep listening to your soul.... You have already found your passion and you will live it till you keep expressing your soul through your passionate writings. But as the Zen Masters say, make sure that hereafter you live your life as if work is play and play is work. And the day you find yourself alienated from this practice, you will see yourself being driven again by nonsensical and deceptive challenges posed by extrinsic anchors and envious benchmarks. This is exactly when your soul will again strange itself from you and you will be pushed back to your days of distress and despair."

Though I considered my life's experiences to be my principal master, I saw in Dr. Sapatnekar the *guru* who mentored my wandering self to imbibe the ability to appreciate the significance of what I had experienced in my life. I remembered Maya's thoughts on the uniqueness of every soul and the non-existence of fixed formulas for attaining completeness and thanked Dr. Sapatnekar for guiding my way to my life of passion through my soul.

Following Dr. Sapatnekar's mantra of work and play, I took up several new projects at work. I was not scared to take risks and experiment. I took up the complete responsibility of my company's sales operations in South East Asia and initiated and implemented newer models for reaching out to newer businesses and geographies. In one of those initiatives, I started working towards setting up the *Regional Customer Councils* in each of our focus markets and joined hands with industry experts and influencers to address the emerging needs of specific geographies.

Within a very short while I appointed channel and technology partners in several new markets such as Vietnam, Indonesia and Philippines and kicked off joint campaigns across the region.

Even on the home front, I started spending time on things that I considered immensely close to my soul. I started off with a revival movement in my kitchen, attempting varieties of those wonderful traditional preparations that as a child I used to relish during the summer holidays spent with my grandparents. I began working on the lyrics of all the half-written songs from my college days and started compiling thoughts for my next book. And all along these moments of passion, I lived an exceptionally cherished closeness with Aparoopa, passionately awaiting the arrival of the little soul!

"You are doing a great job, Siddhartha. To tell you the truth, you have always been a good employee, but in the last three months what you have delivered has made you exceptional! I don't know from where all this energy has come in but I must tell you that I am immensely impressed. Keep it up my friend! I wish you all the best from the bottom of my heart! And listen, I want another wonder from you now.... The Board has decided to buy and take over *TechBank Solutions* in Thailand. Khun Sarawut has also expressed his consent. The final talks are on with their board. We hope to close the deal soon. In the first or second week of the next month, I would want you to go to Bangkok again and take charge of the pre-acquisition negotiations from our end. You may look at the entire month of September to finish this job."

On the eleventh of September I flew again to Bangkok. This time it was Sukhon who came to receive me at the airport.

Sukhon was looking amazingly attractive in her black business-suit and the peacock-blue scarf that I had gifted her in my last visit. The pale peach lip-gloss that she was wearing was adding on to her intense sensuality.

We shook hands and quickly got into her car without exchanging too many words. On our way to the hotel I obsessively kept staring at Sukhon as she drove us through the crowded streets of Bangkok. There was nothing much that I could talk to her about and she never looked too keen to start a conversation either.

In the afternoon, as I started sharing my agenda with the team from TechBank Solutions, I noticed Sukhon quietly looking at her own presentation slides without being too affected by the ongoing discussions. She looked disinterested and irritated. It seemed she wasn't really happy about the proposed acquisition.

Later on, in the evening, as the two of us went to the Lumphini Night Bazaar for dinner, she disclosed in a rather contemplative mood that TechBank Solutions was actually founded by her father twenty one years ago in partnership with Khun Sarawut. Six years ago when her father died of a cardiac arrest in Singapore, she was still studying in the US. However, owing to her father's last wish, she discontinued her education and came back to join the company. She shared that she has been persistently objecting to selling the company as she believed that her father's presence was still alive through its very existence....

"Siddhartha, I have heard that a female called Sukhon is creating some problems... I want you to keep a watch on her. Just work with Khun Sarawut and figure out what is the problem with that *bitch*. I have been told that her mother still holds some share in the company. If required just talk to her and tell her that we can work out some attractive deal for her. Got it?"

Kalra was too smart for Sukhon and the deal ultimately *worked out*. Sukhon was offered the position of *Director Marketing—SEA Region* and an assurance that TechBank Solutions would be allowed to retain its original name even after the acquisition.

Our work resumed... everything seemed normal. Sukhon too was seen sufficiently involved. But there was a subtle yet an evident change in her attitude towards me. I was gradually convinced that she was trying to maintain some distance. I didn't bother to dig into it but learnt from Khun Sarawut that she suspected me behind the *conspiracy* of acquiring TechBank Solutions and saw in me a shrewd agent of Kalra in eventually compelling her to sell off her family's most prized possession. The gap between us further widened as we progressed with the acquisition and towards the end of my stay at Bangkok we were not even in talking terms.

I was disturbed by the whole episode and wanted to convince Sukhon of my innocence. I tried on several occasions to persuade her but no luck.... My attempts continued and she remained firm on her stand.

Sukhon's changing attitude towards me came with a surprising rush of unfamiliar and untamed emotions. It was a feeling that I wasn't quite acquainted with. In point of fact, it sensed almost like a mystery that I had to struggle hard to solve and understand.... But evidently, the sense of indifference and revulsion as conveyed by Sukhon's unforgiving behaviour did fuel an astounding obsession within my distressed self that caught me up in the grip of an irresistibly hysterical desire.

I couldn't any more see in her the divine radiance that once distinguished her from the futile glitters of the material world. Even the spiritual serenity in her very presence that once embodied the much sought-after eternal completeness diffused into absolute nothingness. Amidst these altering sensations, deep within my heart, I felt a dominant detestation for Sukhon. And almost around the supposed detestation, I also discovered a covetous craving for her approbation and I ended up longing eccentrically for her, infuriated and instigated by the spur of riotous infatuation.

The pre-acquisition work completed on the eighteenth of October and the very next day I flew back to India without really winning back Sukhon's confidence. It was a serious blow to my male ego and a defeat that I couldn't really swallow with ease. But more than anything else, it was the feeling of rejection that kept bothering me for long!

The passion that of late was driving me ahead in the journey of my soul also gradually started fading away from my life. For weeks together, I was not the same person. I was at work, but not working. I was at home, but not feeling at home. I felt drained-out and sick. I was not alive. There were tremendous demands; both on the personal and the professional fronts..., Apu was at her advanced stage of pregnancy. And Kalra was planning a few product launches in India and Singapore. But I was unconcerned, lost perpetually in depressing thoughts and mechanically performing my *duties* both at home and work.

Meanwhile, Vishwas Deshpande, an ex-colleague of mine, married to one of Aparoopa's closer friends, had started approaching me with a job offer in his recently started company. *Authorhub Global,* the company, was into outsourced authoring services.

Vishwas wanted me to set up his Business Development function and explore projects with online-publication houses in the US.

"Siddhartha, the offer on the face of it might not seem attractive enough.... We are just a start-up and are yet to strike big deals. But I am confident. We will make it big, soon! And with people like you, why not? Look buddy, I don't know about anything else but I can definitely offer you a great future with us. We can work on a profit-sharing basis and once we strike a couple of good deals in the US, money would just flow in.... Besides, we have recently received some VC funding and that would definitely take care of your current salary and stuff.... And what if I say that I am willing to match your current salary and on top of that offer you a certain percentage of profits as well? What say? And hey, just forgot to ask; you have a valid US Business Visa, right?"

Though I always liked Vishwas as a person and was aware of the substantial credibility that he of late had earned in the industry as a progressive entrepreneur, I wasn't quite sure of him as an employer. He had the reputation of being pointlessly shrewd and manipulative without a cause.... And not too many looked upon him as a great people's person either! However, tempted by the brighter prospects of the offer, I decided to mull over it further and didn't communicate my immediate refusal. I kept evaluating and re-evaluating Vishwas' proposal while remembering Apu's warning of not opting for a job that does not free me from my constraints and grant me the required freedom. But considering my ongoing depression I became rather optimistic about the changes that this job could possibly bring in.

With growing thoughts about the change, three long annoying weeks mutely passed by and my *depression* somehow started showing signs of an indolent retreat....

On a moderately brighter autumn morning as I woke up from my tiresome sleep, once again, I realised that I was being paid a yet another visit by my recurrent dream.... But this time, the content of the dream seemed a little unusual.... It started off in the same sequence... I saw that I was sleeping with Maya beside me and a sudden rush of passion turning me into a child. But towards the end, instead of her vanishing into nowhere, I saw her changing into another woman, who quite evidently resembled Sukhon!

I suddenly felt the need to get out of my psychic hibernation. I jumped out of my bed in utter frustration and ran off to the balcony to embrace the rising sun.... As I looked at it and felt its compulsive power within me, I developed an implacable urge to win back my lost self-esteem and once again, almost unknowingly, I found myself getting slowly caught under the gripping influence of *pride* and *greed*.... Once again I felt pulled by the anchors of raw voracity. Once again I was all set to *run with rage*.... But fortunately, this time I didn't miss to hear the voice of my soul.... Yes, it was back... and almost out of the blue, it challenged me with a fresh new reasoning.... I began evaluating the idea of digging out the root of my obsessive pain, the attempt of avoidance of which was compelling me to seek seemingly deceptive extrinsic diversions like the job offer from Vishwas, which itself was emerging as yet another obsession....

Soon, I found myself at the threshold of yet another quest, wanting to ascertain if it was really Sukhon or just the lure of the great illusion that was causing turbulence yet again in my life.... As the first step, I decided to dump the very thought of Sukhon and started focussing on developing a new relationship with the intent of furthering my experiment with *truth*. I evaluated several options, but the only name that sounded strong enough to beat the warmth and attractiveness of Sukhon was that of Dolly.... And I was almost certain that she was the only one!

"Sidddhhaaaaaaarthaaaaaaa...! O......h my god! I..., I never thought that you would actually call up! Hey thanks, but..., I mean, it's so nice of you, oh, I mean... good that you called! Huh! ...By the way... Siddhartha, how have you been? How is Aparoopa? Hey Siddhartha, just give me a second... Let me just get out of this place. I am actually with one of the NGOs here.... Remember, I was telling you about the non-profit I am setting up here? *Actually*, it is in connection with the same project...."

For some reason Dolly sounded nervous. She seemed both excited and scared. I got curious and ended up asking if everything was okay with her.

"Why? Do I sound *not* okay? Well, but tell me what makes you think so? I am an independent woman. I live life on my own terms. I live in the city I love and work for the cause I believe in. Why shouldn't I be okay?"

The phone call with Dolly didn't really take me anywhere. I started wondering if she was indeed the appropriate choice... I contemplated in length to conclude that she was not, for my selection was rather driven by my sheer lack of choice! Annoyed and thoroughly disappointed, I resumed battling hard to figure out names of other women only to further realise that I actually didn't know too many women in this world; and of the very few I knew, not even a single could ever be a possibility! For an instance, I did of course think of Maya but the very thought of dragging her back into the realm of my psychic world seemed weird and depressing and I dropped the idea like a hot potato.

I spent the whole day in dire frustration. I didn't talk to anyone, didn't work for a single hour at a stretch and didn't even go out for lunch with Ninad.

Towards the end of the day, as I was winding up, I got a call on my mobile phone.

"Siddhartha, can we talk now?" It was Dolly....

"In the morning when you called up, I was sitting with the Chief Executive of one of the non-profits here. God, that female was so irritating! You know Siddhartha; I was absolutely *pissed off* with her... These monkeys... they don't even understand the ABCs of managing non-profits and become the chief executives. Hah, just forget them! *Actually*, you know, I was just too thrilled to see you calling but wasn't too sure if I could talk comfortably in her presence. And then you started off with those typical *are-you-okay* type questions.... Tell me why wouldn't I get irritated? Siddhartha, even the other day at Heathrow, when I met you after so many years, you acted so pricy! I thought there would be so much for us to talk about.... But you never really seemed too keen! Seems you don't talk much these days...."

I was wrong. Dolly was indeed the perfect choice! And right from the time I received her phone-call, I was entirely convinced about it all over again! Over the following few weeks, we started spending substantial time on the phone talking to each other, recalling the days of our common past and sharing the mutual admiration that we never had expressed before. It was Dolly who talked most of the time and I just felt good being her only genuine listener. Soon, our conversations began surpassing the boundaries of reminiscence and re-collections; and evidently we found ourselves increasingly indulged in discussing likelihoods and possibilities around our *relationship*. In one of those conversations, Dolly made a remark on Aparoopa, alleging her of a dishonest intrusion and even went up to the extent of confessing that she still hated her for all that she had done! Dolly didn't spare me either. She overtly reminded me how untruthful, insincere and insensitive I was to have dumped her adoration merely for a better-looking and better-dressed Aparoopa!

Dolly's blunt remarks in some peculiar way created a mild resonance within me; and almost inadvertently, I started developing a feeling of genuine fondness for her. The fondness soon grew into a sort of weakness and every day invariably at around five o'clock in the evening, I found myself walking out of the office, locking myself in my car and making long phone-calls to her.

Once again, after fourteen years of cold aloofness, it started feeling *like love, almost like love!* Finally, I was at peace. I was relieved at having discovered that Sukhon and hence her admiration didn't really matter, for now she didn't even exist any more! Consequently, there was no desire, no longing and no craving for her approbation. More importantly, there was no urge to evade her and no necessity of finding external diversions to do so. I was happy... The experiment proved worthwhile... But the success of the experiment left me once again on the brink of a situation from where the way ahead looked a little difficult and dicey... I feared falling for yet another desire. I feared falling in love again... But my soul, which was maintaining a constant watch, as it led my actions all the way through, ultimately spoke up to let me appreciate that acceptance, appreciation or approbation of an individual or the mass is merely a mirage that every man in different stages of his life tends to chase and possess. I closed my eyes in deep reflection and felt engaged in a joyful conversation with my soul as it took me through transcending levels of enlightenment and ecstasy. It made me understand that genuine love, whether for a person or a pursuit, does not seek approbation of any kind. It further revealed that it is the desire for this approbation that jostled me off my life of passion and compelled me yet again to live the life of the ordinary, the one that is characterised by unending craving, gloom and suffering.

'Genuine love does not expect anything but simply grants you the divine radiance that makes every moment of your life complete and meaningful. It just can't be love if there is expectation and the craving for approbation!'

I was just about to have absorbed the golden revelation that my soul fearing further distractions impatiently got into an evident conspiracy with the soul of the universe and laid down its chosen path ahead.... The same evening, after I returned from work, Apu started complaining of restlessness and nausea. She was quiet but she looked sufficiently tense. It was her thirty-third week but it seemed she was already quite prepared for her long-awaited motherhood...

Soon, we were at the hospital enquiring about the resident doctors at the maternity ward. A senior gynaecologist examined

Apu, and at 9:30 p.m., she was asked to get admitted. Almost after an hour, the doctor came and met me and advised us to go for a caesarean section the next morning at nine o'clock.

Apu and I spent the night in a tiny little room at the hospital, half asleep and half awake. At 8:30 a.m., two nurses came and took Apu to the labour-room. The next seventy minutes that I passed in the visitors' lounge were loaded with an outlandish mix of inexplicable emotions.... Every second that I passed in that swarming little space seemed either ecstatically terrific or breathlessly terrifying. I was sweating, shivering and sighing all along. Suddenly, I hear the tapping sound of a lady's approaching steps. It was one of the nurses....

"Mr. Kumar, you can come and see your baby... It's a boy!"

The nurse, holding and lifting the tiny little man in her arms, brought him close to me and my eyes filled with tears of joy that I was deprived of for years together!

"Actually, it is a premature delivery and we will have to keep him under observation for sometime in the Neo Natal-ICU.... Your wife is absolutely fine. We would shift her to the room over an hour's time."

By around eleven, Apu was back in the room. She was not in her complete senses as yet but she managed to smile at me and mumbled a word or two which I knew for sure was no less than telling me that life would now be better than ever before! I went close to her bed and looked at her face which looked complete with contentment and bliss; and all over again I fell in love with the woman who now was the mother of my child!

"Your baby is perfectly fine now. We can get him discharged from the nursery before evening."

At 4:30 p.m., I am at the Neo Natal ICU, trying to peep in from the narrow glass window to catch a glimpse of the tiny soul wrapped in soft old loin-cloth, sleeping charmingly, completely unaware of how cherished and awaited his arrival has been.

And finally by around five, he is with us; rocking quietly on the cradle adjacent to Aparoopa's bed, smiling and wide awake....

I stare at him and he meekly opens his little eyes and looks around; as if trying to acclimatise himself with the people whose destiny has now been anchored to the promise of eternity that he has brought along with him. His innocent and instinctive gestures being so very compelling, I pick him up from the cradle and start sniffing and kissing him impatiently.

I turn to Apu and kiss her forehead with all my warmth. The little man shrieks and diverts all my attention to comfort him.

The phone in my pocket rings, but I am too engrossed to pick it up. It continues ringing and I keep ignoring it till the baby goes quiet. I place him back onto the cradle and pull the phone out from my pocket to see two missed calls; one from Vishwas Deshpande and the other from Dolly. I think for a while and decide not to call them back…, ever.

I pick up the baby from the cradle once again and hold him tenderly in my arms. I look at his radiant face and his sharp blue eyes and pray that he finds in this world true meaning and genuine passion. I close my eyes, kiss him again and decide to name him *Anay*—the one who leads his own way….

Epilogue

INVARIABLY, our lives in this world are driven by some sort of mysterious forces that arise and subsist deep within us. Some of these forces, what we inoffensively call our ill-fate or misfortune, obstinately provoke us to chase illusively unending horizons, diverting us away from the greater purpose of our life, resulting in severe distress and endless frustration.

The characters depicted in this metaphorical fable are essentially the manifestations of some of these forces that human life is ceaselessly influenced and affected by. Though these characters are absolutely fictitious and are purely born out of my mind's eye, in repeated instances, most of them live the forces and the influences that I have witnessed in the lives of the people around me or have personally experienced in my own life. 'Chasing Maya…' is my attempt to proffer a perspective to the soul-in-pursuit-of-true-happiness about transcending the influence of these misleading forces of life.

Among all the characters in the story, the protagonist, Siddhartha Kumar is closest to me. I can relate to quite a few facets of his character…. But largely, he is a representation of the contemporary middle-class urban Indian, who today, in spite of being materially successful, is unhappy, frustrated, disoriented and directionless. I strongly associate with Siddhartha's struggle around overcoming his obstinate complexes. I am fascinated by how, he, encouraged by the series of mystical experiences along his journey of self-quest, discovers that true happiness is his sole aspiration and concludes that a life of passion is the only means to achieve it.

Another character that really intrigues me is that of Baba Menon. Interestingly, like most other characters in the story, he too is a metaphor. He symbolizes the tendencies of stupor and inactivity that can creep into the psyche of any average human being. Nevertheless, he is a wise man, who, along with his eccentric wisdom, prefers to live in a world of his own. Baba Menon's character has been conceived to reflect the intense inertness that the protagonist often experiences due to an apparent lack of a drive or a purpose in life.

Dr. Sapatnekar, on the other hand, happens to be my most adored character.... He reminds me of all those, who, since my very young days, have stood by me and guided my way. Dr. Sapatnekar's character is an archetypical resonance of the protagonist's inherent capacity to lead a life of genuine passion and true happiness based on his very own sense of direction, purpose and drive....

The characters of Maya, Dolly and Sukhon are inspired by my very own interpretation of various incidents of divergence and dilemma intermittently confronted by my friends from both the sexes. Together, the three women represent the multi-faceted anima of the protagonist. While Maya is the personification of the alluring mirage within him that he chases in sheer imprudence, Sukhon and Dolly stand before him as bold question-marks compelling him to seek undeviating solutions to the unresolved conflicts between his soul and his actions.

The simplest and the most truthful character in the entire story is that of Aparoopa. She lives the promise of a life of unadulterated love and true happiness... . I genuinely feel some sort of an innocent pride when at the end of the book she subtly emerges as the source of a serene completeness to the protagonist. The character of Aparoopa is by and large inspired by my wife, Rajeshwari.

Now Available

Fiction Pages 360
978-93-80707-48-8 (HB)
978-93-80707-49-5 (FB)
Price : ₹ 495 (HB) & ₹ 245 (FB)

THE LOST IDENTITY

Quest for the Text of Akbar

(The text which holds the key to the entire Christian Faith)

by Troy Bond

Posing as your murdered friend is never easy! ***The Lost Identity: Quest for the Text of Akbar*** is a spellbinding, action-packed thriller which keeps the readers glued to their seats till the very end. Finding the "Text of Akbar" means illuminating a sacred and extraordinary link to the past that may unlock secrets to the very origins of a world religion. But first he must solve the mystery of who is behind his friend, Dr. Ross's murder, while trying to survive in a palace of easy death.

TALE OF A WASTELAND

English version of highly acclaimed Hindi novel *'Parti:Parikatha'*

by Phanishwar Nath 'Renu'

Fiction Pages 488
978-93-80707-44-0 (HB)
978-93-80707-45-7 (FB)
Price : ₹ 995 (HB) & ₹ 495 (FB)

Phanishwar Nath 'Renu', a true son of the soil, has created in ***Parti Parikatha***, rendered here in English as ***Tale of a Wasteland***—a major modern classic through the original genius he brought to bear upon his theme.

Every reader of this 'epic in prose' will feel real life throbbing and pulsating through each page of this book. On its broad canvas, the life of two generations has been inimitably presented by Renu with his exquisite art which creates unforgettable characters through episodes and dialogues in an idiom that shows his power over words.

Fiction/Art&Music/Romance
Pages 312
978-93-80707-52-5 (HB)
978-93-80707-53-2 (FB)
Price : ₹ 495 (HB) & ₹ 245 (FB)

FANTASIA

ON A THEME OF THOMAS TALLIS

by Vaughn Petterson

Touching on a wide range of different themes, ***Fantasia on a Theme of Thomas Tallis*** is a truly compelling read. Throughout the pages of his thought-provoking novel, author Vaughn Petterson presents readers with a vivid portrait of the best and worst that humanity has to offer, inviting them to form their own conclusions about the respective moral weight of our various social folkways and mores. Written in a deeply lyrical style, Fantasia successfully incorporates the transformative media of art, music, and literature as a figurative backdrop for protagonist's personal metamorphosis.

THE GROWING YEARS

Incidents in the Life of a Family

by Ann Delorme

Fiction Pages 296
978-93-80707-46-4 (HB)
978-93-80707-47-1 (FB)
Price : ₹ 395 (HB) & ₹ 195 (FB)

A quirky and provocative account of an Anglo Indian family residing in a military cantonment, in Central India, in the 1960s.

The Growing Years is a novel that deals with the life of a mother living in the shadow of death and the painful growing years of her pre-teen and young adolescent children. It delves, with a touch of humour, into the complex psychology of adults and children as they age towards maturity and death, unwilling participants.

The novel also deals with an Anglo Indian culture left behind by the colonials who quit India, a culture that has been nurtured and blossoms in the gardens of a hybrid race who still closet themselves in the bungalows of their minds.

Now Available

A CODER'S COCKTAIL

What Not to Do in IT...

by Shashwat Rai

Fiction Pages 238
978-93-80707-14-3 (HB)
978-93-80707-15-0 (FB)
Price : ₹ 595 (HB) & ₹ 345 (FB)

We have all read about what not to do in the IITs, even watched the blockbuster movie on what not to do in normal engineering colleges. Wonder why no one told us about what to do once you graduate and get in a job, or what not to do in IT?

Set in times of recession, on the backdrop of the most respected IT company of India, this story will take you on an epic tale of friendship and betrayal, of love and office politics traversing on its way the gloomy shades of today's youth to the age old struggles of seeking to answer the dark side of being a man.

SHE

Stories of Modern Indian Women

by Dixy Gandhi

Fiction/Stories, Pages 190
978-81-909013-1-4 (HB)
978-93-80707-22-8 (FB)
Price : ₹ 425 (HB) & ₹ 245 (FB)

Society in modern times is changing very fast, and so is changing the situation and role of women in facing and dealing with them. With the expansion of education among them, they are taking things with gusto and intelligence, at times coming out with unexpected results.

It is time women wrote with themselves at the centre of happenings. ***SHE*** is a collection of stories that describe the lives of independent, single individuals who are too arrogant to be dragged down by mediocrity. Every story is an effort to understand a central theme which defines the story.

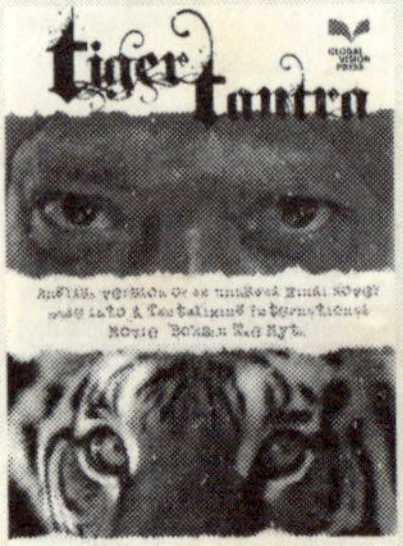

TIGER TANTRA

English version of an unusual and highly acclaimed Hindi novel '*Mrigaantak*'

by Ganga Prasad Vimal

Fiction Pages 186
978-93-80707-00-6 (HB)
978-93-80707-12-9 (FB)
Price ₹ 425 (HB) & ₹ 245 (FB)

Tantra is an aspect of the many-sided Hindu religion, the most mysterious as also practiced in various ways since ancient times. In many regions it touches daily life—such as in the hills of northern India. The Bokshu Vidya or the Tiger-Tantra changes its practitioner into a Tiger, in the process of making him immortal—nothing less. The mantra is lying hidden under tne ruins of a deserted village temple, a scholar is searching for it, a swami is practicing it and using a virgin young girl to make it succeed—and well, the story unfolds…

THE KINDLING TOUCH

The Marie Curie Story of Struggle, Love, Sacrifice and Highest Science

by Debabrata Dasgupta

Biographies Pages 156
978-81-909013-0-7 (HB)
978-93-80707-20-4 (FB)
Price ₹ 295 (HB) & ₹ 195 (FB)

A biographical novel on an extraordinary Polish girl—whose father lost his teaching job, mother died of tuberculosis, she herself lost two governess' jobs, came to Paris to study Physics, worked in a shoddy shed as her laboratory—won her first Nobel Prize, along with her husband Pierre Curie, for the discovery of Radium.

It is not all to describe Madame Curie simply as a devoted scientist; she is a radiant milestone in the realm of modern science. Her whole life carries a divine message. In her life she ventured forward with resolution and courage and finally reached her glorious destination.